This book
was presented

to

_____

by

_____

on

_____

Christmas
TREASURY

DALMATIAN PRESS

CHRISTMAS TREASURY

COPYRIGHT © 2008 DALMATIAN PRESS, LLC

Compiled and edited by Kathryn Knight
Christmas carols illustrated by Ruth Palmer
Vintage sections illustrated by McLouglin Bros. in 1901

Published in 2008 by Dalmatian Press, LLC.
The DALMATIAN PRESS name is a trademark
of Dalmatian Publishing Group, LLC, Franklin, Tennessee 37067.

ISBN: 1-40375-005-X
17522-0608

08 09 10 11 SFD 10 9 8 7 6 5 4 3 2 1

Through
poems and carols
and stories old and new,

we wish you and your family
a very merry Christmas—

this year, next year
and for many years
to come.

The Contents

Moore is thought to have written "A Visit from Saint Nicholas" on Christmas Eve, 1822, while traveling home by sleigh through the snowy New York streets, Christmas turkey in hand. His plump, bearded Dutchman sleigh driver became the "right jolly old elf" who delighted Moore's six children that night as he read them his whimsical poem.

Almost 200 years later, parents still tuck their children into bed on Christmas Eve with this classic Christmas tale of cheer and wonder.

The Night Before
Christmas

Clement Clarke Moore
Illustrated by Tom Newsom

'Twas the night before Christmas,
    when all through the house
Not a creature was stirring,
    not even a mouse.

The stockings were hung
    by the chimney with care,
In hopes that St. Nicholas
    soon would be there.

The children were nestled
all snug in their beds,
While visions of sugarplums
danced in their heads.

And Mamma in her 'kerchief,
and I in my cap,
Had just settled down
for a long winter's nap,

When out on the lawn
   there arose such a clatter,
I sprang from the bed
   to see what was the matter.

Away to the window
   I flew like a flash,
Tore open the shutters,
   and threw up the sash.

The moon on the breast
   of the new-fallen snow
Gave the luster of midday
   to objects below,

When, what to my wondering
eyes should appear,
But a miniature sleigh
and eight tiny reindeer,

With a little old driver,
so lively and quick,
I knew in a moment
it must be St. Nick.

More rapid than eagles
his coursers they came,
And he whistled, and shouted,
and called them by name:

"Now, Dasher! now, Dancer! now, Prancer and Vixen!

On, Comet! on, Cupid! on, Donder and Blitzen!

To the top of the porch!
to the top of the wall!
Now, dash away! dash away!
dash away, all!"

As dry leaves that before
   the wild hurricane fly,
When they meet with an obstacle,
   mount to the sky,

So up to the housetop
   the coursers they flew,
With the sleigh full of toys,
   and St. Nicholas too.

And then, in a twinkling,
I heard on the roof
The prancing and pawing
of each little hoof.

As I drew in my head,
and was turning around,
Down the chimney St. Nicholas
came with a bound.

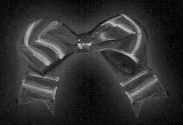

He was dressed all in fur,
    from his head to his foot,
And his clothes were all tarnished
    with ashes and soot.

A bundle of toys
    he had flung on his back,
And he looked like a peddler
    just opening his pack.

His eyes—how they twinkled!
   his dimples—how merry!
His cheeks were like roses,
   his nose like a cherry!

His droll little mouth
   was drawn up like a bow,
And the beard of his chin
   was as white as the snow.

The stump of a pipe
   he held tight in his teeth,
And the smoke it encircled
   his head like a wreath.

He had a broad face
   and a little round belly
That shook when he laughed,
   like a bowlful of jelly.

He was chubby and plump—
  a right jolly old elf;
And I laughed when I saw him,
  in spite of myself.

A wink of his eye
  and a twist of his head
Soon gave me to know
  I had nothing to dread.

He spoke not a word,
  but went straight to his work,
And filled all the stockings—
  then turned with a jerk;

And laying his finger
  aside of his nose,
And giving a nod,
  up the chimney he rose!

He sprang to his sleigh,
   to his team gave a whistle,
And away they all flew
   like the down of a thistle.

But I heard him exclaim,
   ere he drove out of sight:

"Happy Christmas to all,

and to all a good night!"

Up on the Housetop

Words and Music: Benjamin R. Hanby

Up on the house - top, rein - deer pause;
First comes the stock - ing of lit - tle Nell.
Next comes the stock - ing of lit - tle Will.

Out jumps good ol' San - ta Claus!
Oh, dear San - ta, fill it well.
Oh, just see what a glo - rious fill!

Down through the chim - ney with lots of toys, All for the lit - tle ones'
Give her a dol - ly that laughs and cries; One that will o - pen and
Here is a ham - mer and lots of tacks; Al - so a ball and a

Christ - mas joys! Ho, ho, ho! Who wouldn't go?
shut her eyes.
whip that cracks!

Ho, ho, ho! Who would-n't go_____ Up on the house - top,

click, click, click! Down through the chim - ney with ol' Saint Nick!

On the twelfth day

of CHRISTMAS my true love gave to me:

TWELVE drummers drumming

ELEVEN pipers piping

TEN lords a-leaping

NINE ladies dancing

EIGHT maids a-milking

SEVEN swans a-swimming

SIX geese a-laying

FIVE golden rings

FOUR calling birds

THREE French hens

TWO turtledoves

and a partridge in a pear tree!

THE TWELVE DAYS OF CHRISTMAS is a traditional carol celebrating the twelve days between CHRISTMAS and EPIPHANY, January 6.

41

The Magic of Santa Claus

Here's a nice little story for good girls and boys,
All about Santa Claus, Christmas and toys...

THE top of the Earth, which is called the North Pole,
Is where Santa Claus lives, a right jolly old soul!
About him the snow lies so thick on the ground
That the sun cannot melt it the
whole summer round.

His twinkling eyes are so merry and bright,
That they sparkle like two little stars in the night.
He has rosy cheeks and the snowiest hair,
Though the top of his head is quite shiny and bare.

And each Christmas Eve, from his toes to his chin,
Santa's bundled up tight so the cold can't creep in.
His deer from the mountains are harnessed with care,
As they anxiously prance in the clear, frosty air.

Santa cracks his long whip
and whistles a tune,
Then he winks at the stars
and he nods to the moon.
And up, up away they soar,
picking up speed,
For their magical journey
each Christmas Eve.

On a starry night in December, Santa's trip begins.

The reindeer take flight
with lightning-fast speed.
In fact, they're so fast,
you'd swear they had wings!
And these glorious reindeer
can easily fly
To the top of a roof,
no matter how high.

Then, down, down the chimney
Santa descends,
With a snap of his fingers,
a wink and a grin.
He has to be quick, to be through in a night.
His gifts must arrive before first-morning light!

So he fills up the stockings with trinkets and toys,
All without making the teeniest noise.
And with tinkling bells, on each snowy rooftop,
The proud reindeer wait—and keep the night watch.

Down, down the chimney, Santa descends.

A Wondrous Christmas Eve

Santa is cheerful but pleasantly shy.
(He likes to do all his good deeds on the sly.)
So there's no use in spoiling a long winter's nap
Attempting a peek at this jolly old chap.

No, when Christmas Eve comes you must slip into bed,
Pull up the covers and lay down your head.
Then Santa arrives with his magical pack—
A bag full of playthings slung over his back!

He gives to young children who live *everywhere*,
And the rich and the poor are alike in his care.
So great is his love for all girls and boys
That making them happy is what he enjoys.

Watching and waiting for Santa's sleigh.

W elcome to
the world of
The Nutcracker,
a place of wonder
and toys and treats,
where young Marie
becomes a Queen,
and dreams and
wishes come true.

Adapted from the original story,
The Nutcracker and the Mouse King,
written in 1816 by the German
author E.T.A. Hoffmann.

THE
NUTCRACKER

From the original story by E.T.A. Hoffmann

Adapted by Bethany Snyder
Illustrated by Pat Thompson

Christmas Eve! No other evening is *so* exciting (as I'm sure you'll agree). Marie, who was seven years old, was eagerly awaiting the magic of Christmas Eve. She and her older brother Fritz had been listening to the comings and goings and strange noises from the living room all day. Fritz had even spied a dark, hunched man coming from the living room. This could only be their godfather, Papa Drosselmeier.

At last, after a whole day
of listening and waiting
and nearly bursting with
excitement, Marie and her
brother were allowed into
the living room. And what
do you think they saw
when they came through
the door? Why, just the
most beautiful, shining
Christmas tree that
ever was.

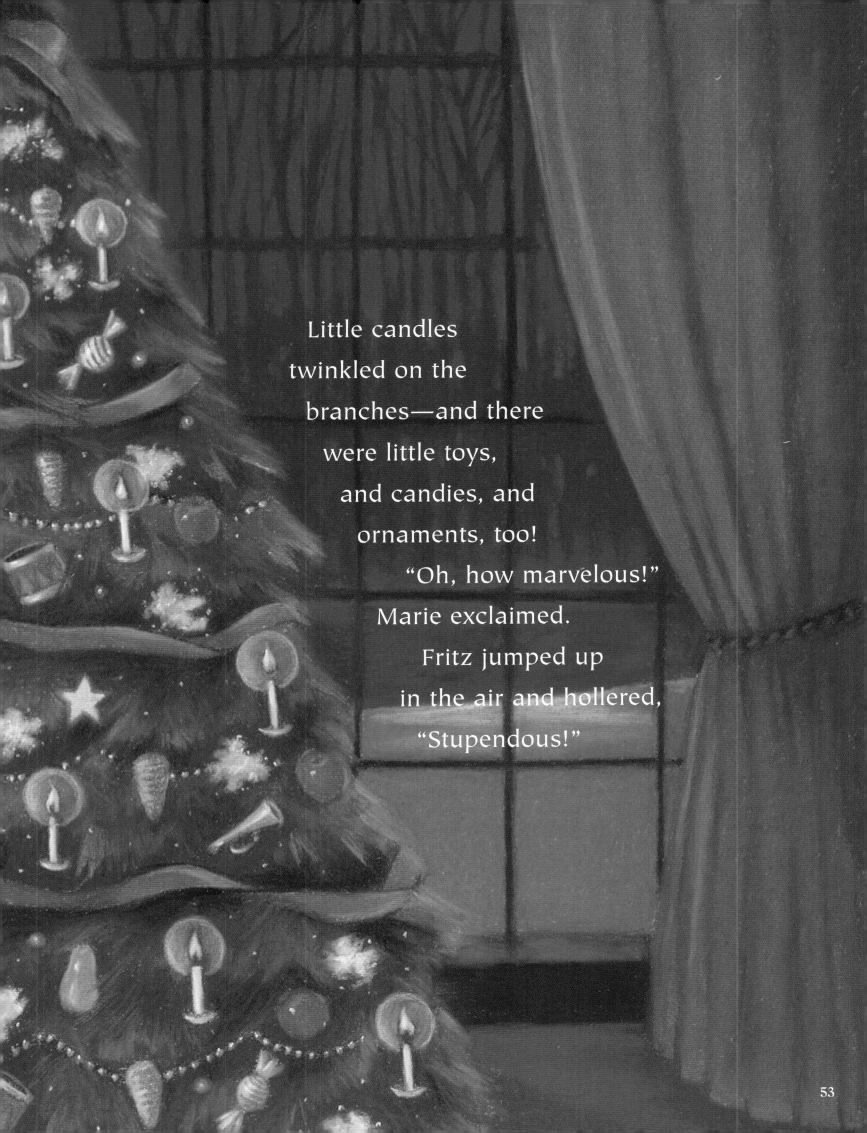

Little candles
twinkled on the
branches—and there
were little toys,
and candies, and
ornaments, too!
"Oh, how marvelous!"
Marie exclaimed.
Fritz jumped up
in the air and hollered,
"Stupendous!"

And what was over here? A wooden horse for Fritz (who simply adored horses) and a whole new set of soldiers for his army. For Marie there was a new doll (Marie immediately named her Clara, because no doll should have to go very long without a proper name), and the most beautiful dress in all the world, with colored ribbons and buttons.

And then Papa Drosselmeier came into the room
with a splendid surprise—a wonderful castle with
golden towers and sparkling windows! And there was
a tiny Papa Drosselmeier, no taller than your finger,
which appeared at the castle door—going out and
going in again.

The grown-ups oohed and ahhed over the castle.
Marie, who was a polite little girl, thanked her godfather
for the castle before going to play with her new doll.

Marie was just bending over to pick up Clara when she spied a little man hiding under the lowest branches of the tree. "Father, whom does that little man belong to?" Marie asked.

"He is Nutcracker, and he belongs to everyone. Let me show you what he can do."

Father picked up the odd-looking man. He put an almond between the little man's teeth, pulled down on Nutcracker's short wooden cape, and — *Crack!* — pieces of shell fell away and Father handed the nut to Marie.

"Wonderful!" she said. "He is an adorable little man."

"Well," said Father, "since you love him so dearly already, I will place him in your keeping. Of course, you must share him with Fritz."

"Oh, I will!" said Marie, as she hugged the strange wooden man.

Marie put only the softest and smallest nuts in Nutcracker's mouth. She did not want to ruin his big smile or his wide, white teeth.

"Let me see!" a voice demanded.

Marie turned to see Fritz, who grabbed Nutcracker from his sister's hands. He started feeding Nutcracker the very hardest nuts! Nutcracker's teeth gave in with a terrible crunch and three teeth popped out onto the floor.

Poor Nutcracker! He looked so fine in his uniform and shiny black boots—but he had a broken jaw.

"You give him back!" Marie said. She took Nutcracker in her arms. "You are a terrible monster, Fritz."

"I don't know why you would like such an ugly old thing anyway," said Fritz.

"Well, I do!" Marie cried. "I'm going to take care of him and make him better."

She bandaged his broken jaw with a ribbon of silk from her new dress. Then she took her wounded Nutcracker to the large glass cabinet in the living room, where they kept their favorite dolls and toys.

Marie looked at Clara. "I'm sorry, Clara," she said, "but Nutcracker is badly wounded, and I know you won't mind giving up your bed to him, now, will you?" (Clara did not mind.) "Very good. Now, rest well, Nutcracker. It is late. Papa Drosselmeier will fix your teeth and jaw tomorrow and you'll be good as new."

As Marie turned to go upstairs to bed, the tall grandfather clock chimed the midnight hour. Then the strangest thing happened. Marie heard squeakings and clatterings behind her. She spun around, and—could it be? Hundreds of mice were pouring out from under the sofa and chairs, and from between the cracks in the doors!

And then a terrible rumbling shook the floor, and up came a giant Mouse King with seven heads! And on those heads were seven gold crowns!

"I've come for Nutcracker and he will be mine!" he shouted.

Nutcracker leaped
from the glass cabinet,
leading Fritz's toy
soldiers! The army
fought bravely—
shooting gumdrop cannonballs at the awful mice. But the Mouse
King suddenly sprang at Nutcracker!

"Stay away from him!" Marie shouted.

She threw her left shoe into the fray—and it hit the Mouse King
right on his many heads. He ran away with all the other mice.
Well, Marie fainted right then and there.

Marie awoke in her very own bed. Had it all been a dream? She looked up and saw Papa Drosselmeier smiling gently at her.

"I have something for you, my dear…"

And do you know what it was? Why, it was Nutcracker! And he was mended! His teeth were in straight and his jaw worked perfectly. Marie hugged him tightly. She had tears in her eyes as she thanked her dear Papa Drosselmeier.

That night, Marie couldn't sleep. Just after the clock chimed midnight, she heard strange sounds—clanging and crashing from the living room!—then a terrible squeak!—then a knock on the bedroom door!—and then a voice crying, "Marie! Open the door. I have wonderful news!"

Marie recognized the voice of Nutcracker and let him in.

"I have defeated the Mouse King!" Nutcracker exclaimed. "It was you who gave me the courage to defeat that nasty creature. To thank you, I wish to give you these."

He handed her seven tiny gold crowns. Marie clasped her hands together with delight.

"I must tell you, dear Marie, that I am really a king," said Nutcracker. "A king of the most wondrous land in all the world! Toyland! And now, will you join me as I travel to my kingdom to celebrate this happy occasion?"

Marie could think of nothing she would rather do.

Marie followed Nutcracker to the front closet, where Nutcracker revealed a hidden ladder. Marie was *just* small enough to climb up this ladder, and soon found herself standing in a sweet-smelling meadow.

"This is Candy Meadow," said Nutcracker. "Now we will travel though all of Toyland on our way to Marzipan Castle in the City of Sweets. That is where I live."

Oh, and Toyland was marvelous! They passed through Almond and Raisin Gateway. They watched a charming ballet. They went by Orange Brook and River Lemonade, and past Gingerbread City on the Honey River. In each of these places, Marie saw the most amazing things: houses and whole villages made out of all manner of sweets, and the friendliest people you could ever hope to meet. There were creatures of all kinds, and they were dancing and laughing about in the merriest way.

They finally came to a rose-colored lake. Nutcracker summoned a jeweled gondola pulled by dolphins to take them across the water.

On and on, under a moonlit sky, they glided over the lake. There ahead lay the City of Sweets and Marzipan Castle! When they arrived, what do you think Marie saw? Only the most beautiful houses, all made of brightly-colored candies, and a marketplace full of delicious sweets that made her mouth water.

Nutcracker took Marie up to his castle, where she met all the ladies of the house, and the royal pages and such. Everyone was so nice that Marie decided she would *never* leave.

They had a wonderful meal of hundreds of candies and desserts. And then Marie started to yawn and rub her eyes. Can you blame her? She had been through quite a bit of excitement, to say the least (and she had probably eaten a bit too much candy). Indeed, Marie *did* fall fast asleep to the sound of her beloved Nutcracker talking…

…and when she awoke, she was in her own bed.

"Oh, it just couldn't have been a dream!" she said sadly.

But what was this in her hand? Why, the seven tiny gold crowns that Nutcracker had given her.

Many, many years later, Marie sat in the living room, gazing at her old, beloved Nutcracker in the glass cabinet.

"Oh, Nutcracker," she said, "if only you were really alive. I would love you just as you are! I don't think you are ugly. I think you are handsome."

Just then Marie's mother came in. "Sit up like a proper young lady," she said. "Papa Drosselmeier's nephew is here to meet you."

"Who?" said Marie, sitting up very straight indeed.

In came a handsome young man. He smiled, walked over, and took Marie's hand in his own.

"Oh, sweet Marie," he said, "I *am* really alive! You were kind and gentle enough to say that you would love me just as I am... and so, here I am. Now, would you do me the honor of becoming my wife— and queen of all Toyland?"

"Nutcracker—is it really you?" whispered Marie. "Of course I will!"

Ah, dear children, who can say how such things happen in this world— and in the world of toys and dreams? Who can say how love creates its own magic? And who can say whether Queen Marie and her beloved King Nutcracker rule over Toyland to this very day? If you have the eyes and heart for it, dear children, perhaps someday you will visit Toyland—and then... *you* can say.

I Saw Three Ships

Words and Music: William Sandys, 1833

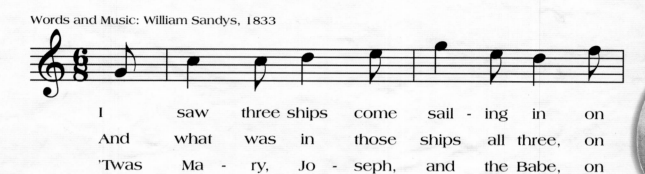

I saw three ships come sail-ing in on
And what was in those ships all three, on
'Twas Ma - ry, Jo - seph, and the Babe, on

Christ - mas Day, on Christ - mas Day. I
Christ - mas Day, on Christ - mas Day? And
Christ - mas Day, on Christ - mas Day. 'Twas

saw three ships come sail - ing in on
what was in those ships all three, on
Ma - ry, Jo - seph, and the Babe, on

Christ - mas Day in the morn - ing.
Christ - mas Day in the morn - ing?
Christ - mas Day in the morn - ing.

Margery Williams'
beloved tale of love,
hope, and compassion
has been delighting
children since its original
publication in 1922.

The Velveteen Rabbit

or

HOW TOYS BECOME REAL

by

MARGERY WILLIAMS

Illustrated by

PAT THOMPSON

There was once a velveteen rabbit, and in the beginning he was really splendid. He was fat and bunchy, as a rabbit should be; his coat was spotted brown and white, he had real thread whiskers, and his ears were lined with pink sateen. On Christmas morning, when he sat wedged in the top of the Boy's stocking, with a sprig of holly between his paws, the effect was charming.

There were other things in the stocking, nuts and oranges and a toy engine, and chocolate almonds and a clockwork mouse, but the Rabbit was quite the best of all. For at least two hours the Boy loved him, and then Aunts and Uncles came to dinner, and there was a great rustling of tissue paper and unwrapping of parcels, and in the excitement of looking at all the new presents the Velveteen Rabbit was forgotten.

FOR A LONG TIME he lived in the toy cupboard or on the nursery floor, and no one thought very much about him. He was naturally shy, and being only made of velveteen, some of the more expensive toys quite snubbed him. The mechanical toys were very superior, and looked down upon everyone else; they were full of modern ideas, and pretended they were real. The model boat, who had lived through two seasons and lost most of his paint, caught the tone from them and never missed an opportunity of referring to his rigging in technical terms. The Rabbit could not claim to be a model of anything, for he didn't know that real rabbits existed; he thought they were all stuffed with sawdust like himself, and he understood that sawdust was quite out-of-date and should never be mentioned in modern circles. Even Timothy, the jointed wooden lion, who was made by the disabled soldiers, and should have had broader views, put on airs and pretended he was connected with Government. Between them all the poor little Rabbit was made to feel himself very insignificant and commonplace, and the only person who was kind to him at all was the Suede Horse.

The Suede Horse had lived longer in the nursery than any of the others. He was so old that his brown coat was bald in patches and showed the seams underneath, and most of the hairs in his tail had been pulled out to string bead necklaces. He was wise, for he had seen a long succession of mechanical toys arrive to boast and swagger, and by-and-by break their mainsprings and pass away, and he knew that they were only toys, and would never turn into anything else. For nursery magic is very strange and wonderful, and only those playthings that are old and wise and experienced like the Suede Horse understand all about it.

"WHAT IS REAL?" asked the Rabbit one day, when they were lying side by side near the nursery fender, before Nana came to tidy the room. "Does it mean having things that buzz inside you and a stick-out handle?"

"Real isn't how you are made," said the Suede Horse. "It's a thing that happens to you. When a child loves you for a long, long time, not just to play with, but REALLY loves you, then you become Real."

"Does it hurt?" asked the Rabbit.

"Sometimes," said the Suede Horse, for he was always truthful. "When you are Real you don't mind being hurt."

"Does it happen all at once, like being wound up," he asked, "or bit by bit?"

"It doesn't happen all at once," said the Suede Horse. "You become. It takes a long time. That's why it doesn't happen often to people who break easily, or have sharp edges, or who have to be carefully kept. Generally, by the time you are Real, most of your hair has been loved off, and your eyes drop out and you get loose in the joints and very shabby. But these things don't matter at all, because once you are Real you can't be ugly, except to people who don't understand."

"I suppose *you* are Real?" said the Rabbit. And then he wished he had not said it, for he thought the Suede Horse might be sensitive. But the Suede Horse only smiled.

"The Boy's Uncle made me Real," he said. "That was a great many years ago; but once you are Real you can't become unreal again. It lasts for always."

The Rabbit sighed. He thought it would be a long time before this magic called Real happened to him. He longed to become Real, to know what it felt like; and yet the idea of growing shabby and losing his eyes and whiskers was rather sad. He wished that he could become it without these uncomfortable things happening to him.

There was a person called Nana who ruled the nursery. Sometimes she took no notice of the playthings lying about, and sometimes, for no reason whatever, she went swooping about like a great wind and hustled them away in cupboards. She called this "tidying up," and the playthings all hated it, especially the tin ones. The Rabbit didn't mind it so much, for wherever he was thrown he came down soft.

ONE EVENING, when the Boy was going to bed, he couldn't find the china dog that always slept with him. Nana was in a hurry, and it was too much trouble to hunt for china dogs at bedtime, so she simply looked about her, and seeing that the toy cupboard stood open, she made a swoop.

"Here," she said, "take your old Bunny! He'll do to sleep with you!" And she dragged the Rabbit out by one ear, and put him into the Boy's arms.

That night, and for many nights after, the Velveteen Rabbit slept in the Boy's bed. At first he found it rather uncomfortable, for the Boy hugged him very tight, and sometimes he rolled over on him, and sometimes he pushed him so far under the pillow that the Rabbit could scarcely breathe. And he missed, too, those long moonlight hours in the nursery, when all the house was silent, and his talks with the Suede Horse. But very soon he grew to like it, for the Boy used to talk to him, and made nice tunnels for him under the bedclothes that he said were like the burrows the real rabbits lived in. And they had splendid games together, in whispers, when Nana had gone away to her supper and left the night-light burning on the mantelpiece. And when the Boy dropped off to sleep, the Rabbit would snuggle down close under his little warm chin and dream, with the Boy's hands clasped close round him all night long.

And so time went on, and the little Rabbit was very happy—
so happy that he never noticed how his beautiful velveteen fur was getting
shabbier and shabbier, and his tail becoming unsewn, and all the pink
rubbed off his nose where the Boy had kissed him.

$\mathcal{S}$PRING CAME, and they had long days in the garden, for wherever the Boy went the Rabbit went too. He had rides in the wheelbarrow, and picnics on the grass, and lovely fairy huts built for him under the raspberry canes behind the flower border. And once, when the Boy was called away suddenly to go to tea, the Rabbit was left out on the lawn until long after dusk, and Nana had to come and look for him with the candle because the Boy couldn't go to sleep unless he was there. He was wet through with the dew and quite earthy from diving into the burrows the Boy had made for him in the flowerbed, and Nana grumbled as she rubbed him off with a corner of her apron.

"You must have your old Bunny!" she said. "Fancy all that fuss for a toy!"

The Boy sat up in bed and stretched out his hands. "Give me my Bunny!" he said. "You mustn't say that. He isn't a toy. He's REAL!"

When the little Rabbit heard that, he was happy, for he knew what the Suede Horse had said was true at last. The nursery magic had happened to him, and he was a toy no longer. He was Real. The Boy himself had said it.

That night he was almost too happy to sleep, and so much love stirred in his little sawdust heart that it almost burst. And into his boot-button eyes, that had long ago lost their polish, there came a look of wisdom and beauty, so that even Nana noticed it next morning when she picked him up, and said, "I declare, if that old Bunny hasn't got quite a knowing expression!"

That was a wonderful Summer!

Near the house where they lived there was a wood, and in the long June evening the Boy liked to go there after tea to play. He took the Velveteen Rabbit with him, and before he wandered off to pick flowers, or play at brigands among the trees, he always made the Rabbit a little nest somewhere among the bracken, where he would be quite cozy, for he was a kind-hearted little boy and he liked Bunny to be comfortable. One evening, while the Rabbit was lying there alone, watching the ants that ran to and fro between his velvet paws in the grass, he saw two strange beings creep out of the tall bracken near him.

They were rabbits like himself, but quite furry and brand-new. They must have been very well made, for their seams didn't show at all, and they changed shape in a queer way when they moved; one minute they were long and thin and the next minute fat and bunchy, instead of always staying the same like he did. Their feet padded softly on the ground, and they crept quite close to him, twitching their noses, while the Rabbit stared hard to see which side the clockwork stuck out, for he knew that people who jump generally have something to wind them up. But he could not see it. They were evidently a new kind of rabbit altogether.

They stared at him, and the little Rabbit stared back. And all the time their noses twitched.

"Why don't you get up and play with us?" one of them asked.

"I don't feel like it," said the Rabbit, for he did not want to explain that he had no clockwork.

"Ho!" said the furry rabbit. "It's as easy as anything," and he gave a big hop sideways and stood on his hind legs.

"I don't believe you can!" he said.

"I can!" said the little Rabbit. "I can jump higher than anything!" He meant when the Boy threw him, but of course he didn't want to say so.

"Can you hop on your hind legs?" asked the furry rabbit.

That was a dreadful question, for the Velveteen Rabbit had no hind legs at all! The back of him was made all in one piece, like a pincushion. He sat still in the bracken, and hoped that the other rabbit wouldn't notice.

"I don't want to!" he said again.

But the wild rabbits have very sharp eyes. And this one stretched out his neck and looked. "He hasn't got any hind legs!"" he called out. "Fancy a rabbit without any hind legs!" And he began to laugh. "I have!" cried the little Rabbit. "I have got hind legs! I am sitting on them."

"Then stretch them out and show me, like this!" said the wild rabbit. And he began to whirl around and dance, till the little Rabbit got quite dizzy.

"I don't like dancing," he said. "I'd rather sit still!"

But all the while he was longing to dance, for a funny new tickly feeling ran through him, and he felt he would give anything in the world to be able to jump about like these rabbits did.

The strange rabbit stopped dancing, and came quite close. He came so close this time that his long whiskers brushed the Velveteen Rabbit's ear, and then he wrinkled his nose suddenly and flattened his ears and jumped backwards.

"He doesn't smell right!" he exclaimed. "He isn't a rabbit at all! He isn't real!"

"I *am* Real!" said the little Rabbit. "I *am* Real! The Boy said so!" And he nearly began to cry.

Just then there was a sound of footsteps, and the Boy ran past near them, and with a stamp of feet and a flash of white tails the two strange rabbits disappeared.

"Come back and play with me!" called the little Rabbit. "Oh, do come back! I *know* I am Real!"

But there was no answer; only the little ants ran to and fro, and the bracken swayed gently where the two strangers had passed. The Velveteen Rabbit was all alone.

"Oh, dear!" he thought. "Why did they run away like that? Why couldn't they stop and talk to me?"

For a long time he lay very still, watching the bracken, and hoping that they would come back. But they never returned, and presently the sun sank lower and the little white moths fluttered out, and the Boy came and carried him home.

Weeks passed, and the little Rabbit grew very old and shabby, but the Boy loved him just as much. He loved him so hard that he loved all his whiskers off, and the pink lining to his ears turned gray, and his brown spots faded. He even began to lose his shape, and he scarcely looked like a rabbit any more, except to the Boy. To him he was always beautiful, and that was all that the little Rabbit cared about. He didn't mind how he looked to other people, because the nursery magic had made him Real; and when you are Real, shabbiness doesn't matter.

*T*HEN, ONE DAY, THE BOY WAS ILL.

His face grew very flushed, and he talked in his sleep, and his little body was so hot that it burned the Rabbit when he held him close.

Strange people came and went in the nursery, and a light burned all night, and through it all the little Velveteen Rabbit lay there, hidden from sight under the bedclothes; and he never stirred, for he was afraid that if they found him someone might take him away, and he knew that the Boy needed him.

It was a long weary time, for the Boy was too ill to play, and the little Rabbit found it rather dull with nothing to do all day long. But he snuggled down patiently, and looked forward to the time when the Boy should be well again, and they would go out in the garden amongst the flowers and the butterflies and play splendid games in the raspberry thicket like they used to. All sorts of delightful things he planned, and while the Boy lay half asleep he crept up close to the pillow and whispered them in his ear. And presently the fever turned, and the Boy got better. He was able to sit up in bed and look at picture books, while the little Rabbit cuddled close at his side. And one day, they let him get up and dress.

It was a bright, sunny morning, and the windows stood wide open. They had carried the Boy out on the balcony, wrapped in a shawl, and the little Rabbit lay tangled up among the bedclothes, thinking.

The Boy was going to the seaside tomorrow. Everything was arranged, and now it only remained to carry out the doctor's orders. They talked about it all, while the little Rabbit lay under the bedclothes, with just his head peeping out, and listened. The room was to be disinfected, and all the books and toys that the Boy had played with in bed must be burned.

"Hurrah!" thought the little Rabbit. "Tomorrow we shall go to the seaside!" For the Boy had often talked of the seaside, and he wanted very much to see the big waves coming in, and the tiny crabs, and the sand castles.

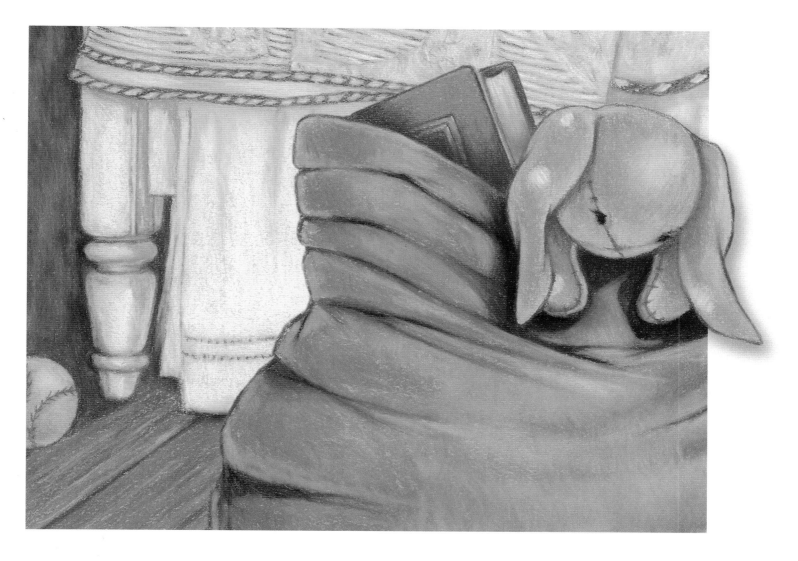

Just then Nana caught sight of him.

"How about his old Bunny?" she asked.

"*That?*" said the doctor. "Why, it's a mass of scarlet fever germs!—Burn it at once. What? Nonsense! Get him a new one. He mustn't have that any more!"

And so the little Rabbit was put into a sack with the old picture books and a lot of rubbish, and carried out to the end of the garden behind the fowl-house. That was a fine place to make a bonfire, only the gardener was too busy just then to attend to it. He had the potatoes to dig and the green peas to gather, but next morning he promised to come quite early and burn the whole lot.

That night the Boy slept in a different bedroom, and he had a new bunny to sleep with him. It was a splendid bunny, all white plush with real glass eyes, but the Boy was too excited to care very much about it. For tomorrow he was going to the seaside, and that in itself was such a wonderful thing that he could think of nothing else.

AND WHILE THE BOY WAS ASLEEP, dreaming of the seaside, the little Rabbit lay among the old picture books in the corner behind the fowl-house, and he felt very lonely. The sack had been left untied, and so by wriggling a bit he was able to get his head through the opening and look out. He was shivering a little, for he had always been used to sleeping in a proper bed, and by this time his coat had worn so thin and threadbare from hugging that it was no longer any protection to him. Nearby he could see the thicket of raspberry canes, growing tall and close like a tropical jungle, in whose shadow he had played with the Boy on bygone mornings.

He thought of those long sunlit hours in the garden—how happy they were—and a great sadness came over him. He seemed to see them all pass before him, each more beautiful than the other: the fairy huts in the flowerbed; the quiet evenings in the wood when he lay in the bracken, and the little ants ran over his paws; the wonderful day when he first knew that he was Real. He thought of the Suede Horse, so wise and gentle, and all that he had told him. Of what use was it to be loved and lose one's beauty and become Real if it all ended like this?

*And a tear, a real tear, trickled down his little shabby velvet nose
and fell to the ground.*

*A*ND THEN A STRANGE THING HAPPENED. For where the tear had fallen a flower grew out of the ground—a mysterious flower, not at all like any that grew in the garden. It had slender green leaves the color of emeralds, and in the center of the leaves a blossom like a golden cup. It was so beautiful that the little Rabbit forgot to cry, and just lay there watching it. And presently the blossom opened, and out of it there stepped a fairy.

She was quite the loveliest fairy in the whole world. Her dress was of pearl and dewdrops, and there were flowers round her neck and in her hair, and her face was like the most perfect flower of all. And she came close to the little Rabbit and gathered him up in her arms and kissed him on his velveteen nose that was all damp from crying.

"Little Rabbit," she said, "don't you know who I am?"

The Rabbit looked up at her, and it seemed to him that he had seen her face before, but he couldn't think where.

"I am the nursery magic Fairy," she said. "I take care of all the playthings that the children have loved. When they are old and worn out, and the children don't need them anymore, then I come and take them away with me and turn them into Real."

"Wasn't I Real before?" asked the little Rabbit.

"You were Real to the Boy," the Fairy said, "because he loved you. Now you shall be Real to everyone."

And she held the little Rabbit close in her arms and flew with him into the wood.

IT WAS LIGHT NOW, for the moon had risen. All the forest was beautiful, and the fronds of the bracken shone like frosted silver. In the open glade between the tree trunks the wild rabbits danced with their shadows on the velvet grass, but when they saw the Fairy they all stopped dancing and stood round in a ring to stare at her.

"I've brought you a new playfellow," the Fairy said. "You must be very kind to him and teach him all he needs to know in Rabbitland, for he is going to live with you for ever and ever!"

And she kissed the little Rabbit again and put him down on the grass.

"Run and play, little Rabbit!" she said.

But the little Rabbit sat quite still for a moment and never moved. For when he saw all the wild rabbits dancing around him he suddenly remembered about his hind legs, and he didn't want them to see that he was made all in one piece. He did not know that when the Fairy kissed him that last time she had changed him altogether. And he might have sat there a long time, too shy to move, if just then something hadn't tickled his nose, and before he thought what he was doing he lifted his hind toe to scratch it.

And he found that he actually had hind legs! Instead of dingy velveteen he had brown fur, soft and shiny, his ears twitched by themselves, and his whiskers were so long that they brushed the grass. He gave one leap and the joy of using those hind legs was so great that he went springing about the turf on them, jumping sideways and whirling round as the others did, and he grew so excited that when at last he did stop to look for the Fairy she had gone.

He was a Real Rabbit at last, at home with the other rabbits.

*A*UTUMN PASSED AND WINTER, and in the Spring, when the days grew warm and sunny, the Boy went out to play in the wood behind the house. And while he was playing, two rabbits crept out from the bracken and peeped at him. One of them was brown all over, but the other had strange markings under his fur, as though long ago he had been spotted, and the spots still showed through. And about his little soft nose and his round back eyes there was something familiar, so that the Boy thought to himself:

"Why, he looks just like my old Bunny that was lost when I had scarlet fever!"

But he never knew that it really was his own Bunny, come back to look at the child who had first helped him to be Real.

May all your
Christmas stockings
be graced with gifts
that bring love and hope
all the new year—
and for years to come.

Deck the Halls

Traditional Welsh Carol

Deck the halls with boughs of hol-ly! Fa la la la la, la la la la.
See the blaz-ing Yule be-fore us. Fa la la la la, la la la la.
Fast a-way the old year pas-ses. Fa la la la la, la la la la.

'Tis the sea-son to be jol-ly. Fa la la la la, la la la la
Strike the harp and join the chor-us! Fa la la la la, la la la la
Hail the new, ye lads and las-ses. Fa la la la la, la la la la

Don we now our gay ap-pa-rel. Fa la la, la la la, la la la
Fol-low me in mer-ry meas-ure, Fa la la, la la la, la la la
Sing we joy-ous all to-geth-er, Fa la la, la la la, la la la

Troll the an-cient Yule-tide ca-rol. Fa la la la la, la la la la
While I tell of Yule-tide treas-ure. Fa la la la la, la la la la
Heed-less of the wind and weath-er. Fa la la la la, la la la la

Christmas wishes sent special delivery.

Letters to Santa Claus

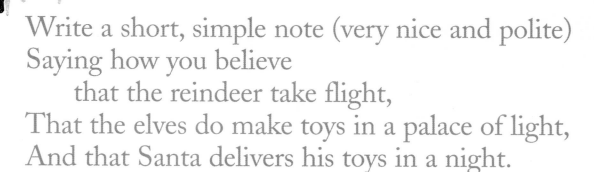

THE letters to Santa
  composed Christmas Eve,
Can be sent to him magically
  up the chimney!

Write a short, simple note (very nice and polite)
Saying how you believe
  that the reindeer take flight,
That the elves do make toys in a palace of light,
And that Santa delivers his toys in a night.

And list what you'd like to find under the tree
The very next morning. (Oh! what you'll see!)
  It's not like dear Santa to ever object
    To hearing of presents that children expect!

Out the chimney your letter
  will float on the air,
    And Santa Claus' helpers
      will capture it there.

Then they'll bustle
  right up to the
  Pole with great speed,
    Delivering letters to
      Santa to read.

The Spirit of Christmas

The most wondrous presents
    and toys are designed
For good little children,
    the gentle and kind.
And when Christmas comes round,
    as it does once a year,
It's certain that Santa will somehow appear!

How funny he looks as he sits on the floor,
Pulling out toys and then searching for more.
His cheeks are flushed pink and his eyes starry bright—
He certainly makes quite a comical sight.

His elves help him make such incredible things—
Monkeys and acrobats jumping on strings,
Footballs and baseballs and mystery games,
Chocolates and lockets and sweet candy canes.

And, oh! the dear dollies with long, curly hair,
That open their eyes or sit up in a chair;
With jackets and socks and the tiniest shoes,
And ribbons and hair clips that doll-babies use.

All the long year, with his paint and his glue,
Santa is making these presents for you!

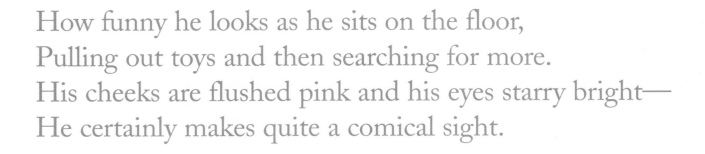

Dollies with petticoats, buttons and bows.

SANTA CLAUS'S PALACE AND TOY FACTORY.

The Crystal Toy Factory

To have enough playthings to fill up his sleigh,
Santa must work with his elves every day.
His workshop's a factory, so grand and so fair—
A real crystal palace set high in the air!
The walls are constructed of crystalline ice
That outshines the rays of the big Northern Lights.
And inside these bustling rooms all day long,
The elves do their work while they sing merry songs.

These good-hearted helpers know
    just how to make...
Trumpets and swords and the best roller skates.
Trains that can run on the tiniest tracks.
Soccer balls, marbles and fun jumping jacks.
Paint boxes, crayons and birds that take flight.
Puzzles and books to be seized with delight.
Soldiers and horses and pull-toys galore...

...Are hammered and sanded
    and sent out
    the door!

The workshop is such a wondrous place.

Toys and Treasures

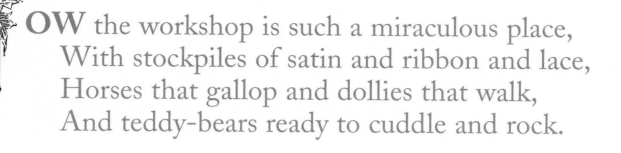

NOW the workshop is such a miraculous place,
With stockpiles of satin and ribbon and lace,
Horses that gallop and dollies that walk,
And teddy-bears ready to cuddle and rock.

Games for all seasons, scooters and kites,
And books that talk back or pop up—what a sight!
Too many baseballs and footballs to count,
And two-wheeled, red bicycles ready to mount.

There are farmyards complete with their fences and trees.
Cows, sheep and oxen, all standing at ease.
Turkeys and ducks and fine chickens and hens,
And dear little piggies to put in their pens.

Each Noah's Ark is sent on its way
With nice little animals, ready to play.
Lions and tigers and camels and bears—
Two of each kind, since they travel in pairs!

Santa's List

Just in case you're longing to know,
These are the virtues good children must show:

Be hard-working at school
    and gentle at play,
Respectful to others,
    and kind through the day.

Not angry or sullen,
    snobbish or curt.
Not one to call names
    or say things to hurt.

Obedient, cheerful,
    and eager to please.
Not one to whine, or tell lies, or tease.

A child who has opened
    his heart to believe
That it's truly more blessed
    to give than receive.

Santa makes his list.

Jolly Old Saint Nicholas

Words and Music: Anonymous
often attributed to Benjamin R. Hanby

Jol - ly old Saint Nich-o-las, Lean your ear this way.
John-ny wants a pair of skates, Su - zy wants a sled;

Don't you tell a sin-gle soul What I'm going to say.
Nel - lie wants a pic-ture book, Yel - low, blue, and red.

Christ-mas Eve is com-ing soon; Now, you dear old man,
Now I think I'll leave to you What to give the rest.

Whis - per what you'll bring to me; Tell me, if you can.
Choose for me, dear San - ta Claus; You will know the best.

A Christmas tale by the Brothers Grimm
Retold by Milo Winter and illustrated by Kitty Diamantes

THE ELVES AND THE SHOEMAKER

THERE WAS ONCE A SHOEMAKER who had become so poor that at last he found he had enough leather left to make only one pair of shoes. So he cut out the leather for the shoes he would make the next day, and after saying his prayers, he went to bed.

In the morning he went down to his shop to begin work, and there on the worktable was the most beautiful pair of shoes. Every stitch was perfect. He had never seen such fine work. He thought they were far more beautiful than any shoes he could ever make.

That very day a man came into the shop and was so delighted with the shoes that he bought them at once, and even paid more for them than the shoemaker had asked. With this money the shoemaker went out and bought enough leather to make two more pairs of shoes.

That evening the shoemaker again carefully cut the leather and laid it out ready for the next day. Then he said his prayers and went to bed.

When the shoemaker came down the next morning, he again found that his work was already done. There on his worktable were two new pairs of shoes, both as beautiful as the first pair. The shoemaker had no trouble selling these shoes, and once again he was paid more money than he had asked. With the money he bought leather for four pairs of shoes. The same wonderful thing happened the next day, and the next and the next. Whatever leather the shoemaker cut at night he found as finished shoes the next morning. Soon the shoemaker became quite rich.

Now, one day, as Christmas was approaching, the shoemaker said to his wife, "Why don't we try to find out who is helping us to finish all our shoes?" His wife liked the idea, so that night, after cutting out the leather, they hid themselves in a dark corner of the workshop.

When midnight came, two naked little elves came in, sat down at the worktable, and at once set to work on the shoes. The shoemaker could hardly believe his eyes. With their little hands they hammered and stitched and sewed and did the most wonderful work. In no time at all they were finished. Then they quickly and quietly hurried away.

The next morning the shoemaker's wife said, "These little elves have changed our fortune. They must be very cold without any clothes. I will make them little shirts and little vests, and coats and pants and little hats. I'll even knit them little stockings. And you must make them little shoes."

The shoemaker agreed, and said, "They have done so much for us. It would be nice to do something for them."

So the shoemaker and his wife spent all day working, and when night came they laid out all the little presents on the worktable and went to hide in the corner. As midnight struck, the elves came in. They were very surprised to find no work laid out for them to do. But when they saw all the little clothes laid out instead, how they danced and laughed! There were never such happy little elves. They put on their beautiful new clothes and began to sing:

> *"Now we're such a pretty sight,*
> *Why should we work all night?"*

They danced all over the room—under the table, on top of the bench and then right out the door. The elves never came back, but from that time on the shoemaker always prospered and was never poor again.

THE END

Jingle Bells

Words and Music: James Pierpoint, 1857

The Christmas Snowman

A Tiny Tale by
Diane Sherman

Illustrated by
Sharon Kane

Sammy was a handsome new snowman. Some boys and girls had given him button eyes, a carrot nose, and a derby hat.

"Oh, look!" said Squeaky Squirrel. "A new snowman! And just in time for Christmas!"

"What's Christmas?" asked Sammy.

"Goodness!" exclaimed Squeaky. "You don't know? Why, Christmas is when we give gifts to people and spread good cheer."

"It's a very special time," added Corky Crow. "Everyone decorates with lights and beautiful colors."

Corky swooped low and landed on Sammy's shoulder. "Would you like a Christmas gift?" asked Corky.

"Oh, yes!" said Sammy.

"Hmmm…" thought Corky Crow.

He took off for his favorite spot—the dump. And there he found a pretty wreath that looked like new. He carried it back in his beak and dropped it over Sammy's head.

"Wow! Thank you," said Sammy. "What a nice decoration. I feel very cheery!"

"Hmmm…" thought Squeaky Squirrel.

He scurried back to his hidey-hole in the tree. From deep inside he pulled out a big red bow he had found on the ground.

"Here you are, Snowman," he said. He tucked the ribbon onto Sammy's hat.

The fieldmice heard the fun and came up pushing a shiny gold ball. "We found it last year!" they said.

"Oh, it's beautiful!" said Sammy as they fastened it to his chest. "Thank you, friends. This makes me very happy."

"I feel like dancing," Mamma Mouse said, as she skittered around the others. "How fun it will be when the boys and girls see their snowman— all decorated for Christmas!"

"Hmmm…" thought Sammy. "Come here, Corky," he said. And he whispered something into Corky's ear.

With a flap and a flutter of his wings, Corky flew off. He found the children racing downhill on their sleds. Swooping low, he plucked a mitten from one of the boys.

"Come back, Crow!" the children called.
They grabbed their sleds and took off after Corky.

"Look!" cried one of the girls. "It's a Christmas snowman!"
"Why, that's *our* snowman!" said a big boy. "Someone has decorated Sammy!"

"You know," said one small boy, "this is a gift that someone has given to us. A Christmas gift."

And all the little animals hippity-hopped with happy hearts.

Winter Ditties
from MOTHER GOOSE

Illustrated by Frederick Richardson

CHRISTMAS

Christmas is coming,
    the goose is getting fat.
Please put a penny in
    the old man's hat.
If you haven't got a penny
    a ha'penny will do;
If you haven't got a ha'penny,
    God bless you.

WINTER

Cold and raw the north winds blow
Bleak in the morning early.
All the hills are covered with snow,
And winter's now come fairly.

WHEN THE SNOW IS ON THE GROUND

The little robin grieves
When the snow is on the ground,
For the trees have no leaves,
And no berries can be found.

The air is cold, the worms are hid;
For robin here what can be done?
Let's strow around some crumbs of bread,
And then he'll live till snow is gone.

LITTLE JACK HORNER

Little Jack Horner
Sat in a corner,
Eating a Christmas pie.
He put in his thumb,
And pulled out a plum,
And said: "Oh, what a good boy am I!"

Bitty Elf Helps Out

A TINY TALE BY KATIE KOBBLE

It was Christmas Eve! The elves in Santa's workshop were busy, busy, busy making toys for girls and boys.

But not Bitty Elf. He was too small to hold the tools.

Oh, how he wished he could help paint the red wagons! But only the big-boy elves were given that job.

The grandma elves wanted him to model the doll clothes. Do you think Bitty wanted to do that?

Mrs. Claus asked him to test the candy canes.
That was a yummy job… though he really wanted
to stir the batter…

…but he was too bitty.

When Bitty saw two big-boy elves
pulling pandas up to Santa's sleigh,
he offered to pull some, too.

But Bitty was not strong enough.
The pandas rolled back down the
hill into a jumble.

"Santa Claus," Bitty said with a sniffle, "I want to help. What can I do?"

"Why, you're just the right size to spread Christmas cheer," said Santa kindly. "I bet you can come up with a special way to make the other elves even cheerier."

Bitty looked through Santa's Christmas books. Then he got a great idea! He would not need tools. He would not need a paintbrush or a mixing spoon.

All he needed was paper and crayons to make his own Christmas cards!

Santa was delighted. Did it matter that Bitty could not spell all the words quite right? Not a bit!

"Look, everyone!" called Santa. "Bitty has brightened our day with his own Christmas cards." All the elves sent up a cherry cheer!

"Bitty, you are just the right size to fit into my bag of toys," said Santa. "Would you like to help me deliver toys tonight?"

Do you think Bitty said yes? You bet Bitty did!

Sweet dreams on Christmas Eve.

Dear Santa,

Please bring me my own Christmas tree,
A sweet-smelling cedar,
as big as can be!
With a dusting of snow
and a tiny surprise—
A bird's nest that's tucked away
on the inside!

Miniature pinecones and candles so bright
That they shimmer like ribbons of winter moonlight.
Crystalline snowflakes and silvery bells,
Tinkling just like the giggles of elves.

Bundles of cinnamon tied here and there,
And peppermint candy canes—plenty to share!
Garlands of marzipan, fashioned like fruit,
Sacks of rock candy, and sugar lumps, too.

Gingerbread sentinels all in a row,
Silvery tinsel and walnuts brushed gold,
Ruby red ornaments, shiny and bright,
And a star that will twinkle
with heavenly light.

—A star for the Christ Child,
heaven's true light.

O Christmas Tree (O Tannenbaum)

Traditional German Carol

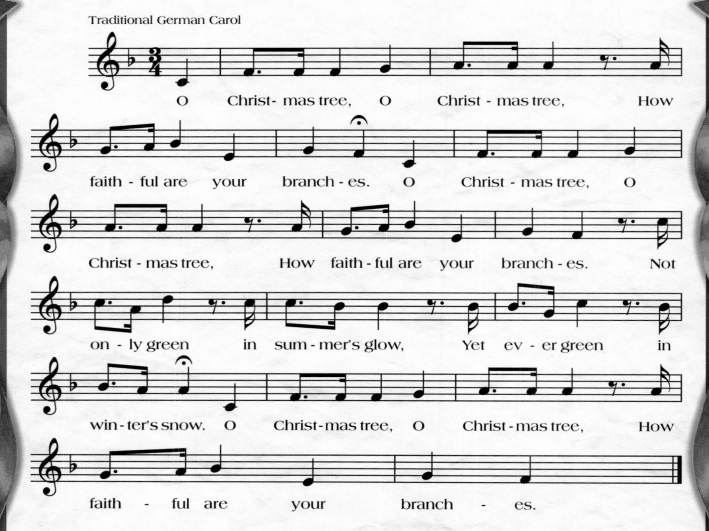

O Christmas tree, O Christmas tree,
You stand so fair and lovely.
O Christmas tree, O Christmas tree,
You stand so fair and lovely.
Your silver star, so pure and bright,
Reflects each tiny candle's light.
O Christmas tree, O Christmas tree,
You stand so fair and lovely.

German:
O Tannenbaum, O Tannenbaum,
Wie treu sind deine Blätter.
O Tannenbaum, O Tannenbaum,
Wie treu sind deine Blätter.

O Christmas tree, O Christmas tree,
You bear a wondrous message.
O Christmas tree, O Christmas tree,
You bear a wondrous message.
You bid us true and faithful be,
And trust in God unchangingly.
O Christmas tree, O Christmas tree,
You bear a wondrous message.

Du grünst nicht nur zur Sommerzeit,
Nein auch in Winter wenn es schneit.
O Tannenbaum, O Tannenbaum,
Wie treu sind deine Blätter.

The Fir Tree

A Christmas tale by Hans Christian Andersen
Adapted by H.P. Paul • Illustrated by Carolyn Ewing

DEEP IN THE FOREST, WHERE THE SUN IS WARM AND THE AIR IS FRESH, grew a fir tree. The sun shone down on the little fir tree. The soft air fluttered its leaves. The little peasant children passed by, chattering merrily. But the fir tree paid no attention, for it was not happy. It wished so much to be tall like its companions, the pines and firs that grew around it.

Sometimes the children would bring large baskets of raspberries or strawberries and would sit near the fir tree and say, "This little tree is the prettiest." This made the fir tree feel even more unhappy than before, so sorry was it to be little.

All the while the tree kept growing a notch or joint taller. As it grew, it complained, "Oh! How I wish I were as tall as the other trees. Then I would spread out my branches on every side, and my top would overlook the wide world. The birds would build their nests on my boughs, and when the wind blew, I would bow with stately dignity like my tall companions."

The tree was so discontented that it took no pleasure in the warm sunshine, the birds, or the rosy clouds that floated over it morning and evening. Sometimes, in winter, when the snow lay white and glittering on the ground, a hare would come springing along and jump right over the little tree. How mortified it would feel!

Two winters passed. The tree had grown so tall that the hare had to run around it. Still the tree remained unsatisfied and would exclaim, "Oh, if I could just keep on growing tall and old! There is nothing else worth caring for in the world!"

Christmastime drew near, and many young trees were cut down. Some were even smaller and younger than the fir tree. These young trees were chosen for their beauty. They were laid on horse-drawn wagons and carried out of the forest.

"Where are they going?" asked the fir tree. "They are not taller than I."

"We know, we know," sang the sparrows. "We have looked in the windows of the houses in the town. We know what becomes of them. They are dressed up in the most splendid manner. We have seen them standing in the middle of a warm room, adorned with honey cakes, gilded apples, playthings, and hundreds of wax candles."

"And then," asked the fir tree, trembling through all its branches, "and then what happens to them?"

"We did not see any more," said the sparrows. "That was enough for us."

"I wonder whether anything so brilliant will ever happen to me," thought the fir tree. "Oh! When will Christmas be here again? I am now as tall and well grown as those who were taken away this year. Oh, that I were now laid on the wagon, or standing in the warm room with all that brightness and splendor around me! Something better and even more beautiful must come after what the sparrows saw, or the trees would not be so decked out. Yes, what follows must be grander and even more splendid. What can it be? I am weary with longing."

"Rejoice with us," said the air and the sunlight. "Enjoy your life in the fresh air."

But the tree would not rejoice, though it grew taller every day. Throughout the winter and summer, its dark-green foliage might be seen in the forest. Passersby would say, "What a beautiful tree!"

A short time before Christmas, the men with the wagons arrived. The fir tree was the first to be cut down. As the axe cut through its stem, the tree fell with a groan to the earth, conscious only of pain and faintness. Its sorrow at leaving its home in the forest was so great that the fir tree forgot how much it had looked forward to this happiness. The tree knew that it would never again see its dear old companions, the trees, nor the little bushes and many-colored flowers that had grown by its side. Perhaps it would never again see the birds as well.

The journey was most unpleasant. The tree had barely recovered  when it, along with several other trees, was unloaded in the courtyard of a house. The first words it heard came from a man, who said, "We only want one, and this is the prettiest."

Then two servants came and carried the fir tree into a large and beautiful home. On the walls hung pictures. Near the great stove stood china vases with lions on the lids. There were rocking chairs, silken sofas, large tables covered with pictures and books, and playthings were all about the floor.

Then the fir tree was placed in a large tub full of sand, which was covered with lovely green felt. The tub itself stood on a very handsome carpet. How the fir tree trembled! What was going to happen now?

It barely had time to wonder when some young ladies arrived, and the servants helped them decorate the tree. On one branch they hung little bags cut out of colored paper. Each bag was filled with candies. On others they hung gilded apples and walnuts, as if they had grown there. All around were hundreds of red, blue, and white candles, which were fastened onto the branches. Dolls exactly like real babies were placed under the green leaves. At the very top was fastened a glittering star made of tinsel. Oh, it was very beautiful!

"This evening," they all exclaimed, "how bright it will be!"

"Oh, that the evening were here," thought the tree, "and the candles lit! Then I shall know what else is going to happen to me. Will the trees of the forest come to see me? I wonder if the sparrows will peep in the windows as they fly by? Shall I grow here in this tub, wearing all these ornaments throughout the year?"

But guessing was of very little use. It made the tree's bark ache, and this pain is as unpleasant for a slender fir tree as a headache is for us. At last the candles were lit, and then what a glow of light the tree presented! It so trembled with joy in all its branches that one of the candles fell among the green leaves and burned some of them.

"Help! Help!" exclaimed the young ladies, but there was no danger, for they quickly extinguished the fire. After this, the tree tried not to hurt any of the beautiful ornaments, even though it was overwhelmed by their brilliancy.

Suddenly the folding doors to the room were thrown open, and a troop of children rushed in. First they were silent with astonishment. Then they shouted for joy. The room rang with their merriment. They danced gaily around the tree, while one treat after another was taken from it. "What are they doing? What will happen next?" wondered the fir tree.

At last the candles burned down to the branches and were put out. Then the children were given permission to plunder the tree. Oh, how they rushed upon it, till some of the branches cracked. Had the tree not been fastened with the glistening star to the ceiling, it would have fallen to the floor. The children then danced about with their pretty toys, and everyone forgot about the tree, except the children's maid, who came and peeped among the branches to see if an apple or a fig had been forgotten.

"A story, a story," cried the children, pulling a little old man toward them.

"Now we shall sit in the shade," the man said, laughing as he seated himself beneath the tree. "I shall only tell one story," he said. "What shall it be?"

The children called this name and that, and there was a great deal of shouting out. At last it was decided that "Humpty Dumpty" was the favorite. The fir tree remained quite still and thought to itself, "Shall I have anything to do with all this?" But the tree had already amused the children as much as they wished.

The old man began the story of Humpty Dumpty—how he fell off the wall and was raised again and married a princess. The children sat quietly and listened. When it was over they clapped their hands and cried, "Tell another, tell another." But the man would not.

After this, the fir tree became quite silent and thoughtful. Never had the birds in the forest told such a tale as "Humpty Dumpty."

"Ah, yes, so this is how it is in the world," thought the fir tree. It believed the whole story because it was told by such a nice man. "Well," the fir tree thought, "who knows? Perhaps I may fall down too, and then I may marry a princess." The fir tree looked forward to the next evening, expecting to be decorated again with lights and playthings, gold and fruit.

"Tomorrow I will not tremble," it thought. "I will enjoy all my splendor. I shall hear a story again, as well." And the tree remained quiet and thoughtful all night. In the morning the servants and the housemaid came in.

"Now," thought the fir tree, "all my splendor is going to begin again." But to its surprise, it was dragged out of the room and up the stairs to the attic. There the tree was thrown on the floor in a dark corner where no daylight shone. And there it was left.

"What does this mean?" thought the tree. "What am I to do here? I can hear and see nothing in a place like this."

The fir tree had plenty of time to think. Days and nights passed, and no one came near it. When at last somebody did come, it was only to put away some large boxes in a corner. So the tree was completely hidden from sight, as if it had never existed.

"It is winter now," thought the tree. "The ground is hard and covered with snow, so no one can plant me. I suppose I shall be sheltered here until spring comes. How thoughtful and kind the people are to me! Still, I wish this place was not so dark and lonely, with not even a little hare to look at. How pleasant it was in the forest, when the snow lay on the ground and a hare would run by—yes, and jump over me, too. Although I did not like it then. Oh! It is terribly lonely here."

"Squeak, squeak," said a little mouse, creeping toward the tree. Then came another, and both of them sniffed at the fir tree and crept between its branches.

"Oh, it is very cold," said the little mouse. "If it were not, we would be quite comfortable here, wouldn't we, old fir tree?"

"I am not old," said the fir tree. "There are many who are older than I."

"Where do you come from? What do you know?" asked the mice, who were full of curiosity. "Have you seen the most beautiful places in the world? Can you tell us all about them? Have you been in the storeroom where cheeses lie on the shelves and hams hang from the ceiling? There you go in thin and come out fat."

"I know nothing of that place," said the fir tree. "But I know the woods where the sun shines and the birds sing."

And then the tree told the little mice all about its youth. They had never heard such an account in their lives. After they had listened attentively, they said, "What a number of things you have seen! You must have been very happy."

"Happy!" exclaimed the fir tree. Then, as it reflected upon what it had been telling the mice, it said, "Ah, yes! After all, those were happy days." And then it went on and related all about Christmas Eve, and how it had been dressed up with candies and apples and lights.

The mice said, "How happy you must have been, old fir tree."

"I am not old at all," replied the tree. "I only came from the forest this winter. I am now checked in my growth."

"What splendid stories you tell," said the little mice.

The next night, four other mice came with them to hear what the tree had to tell. The more it talked, the more it remembered, and then it said, "Those were happy days, but they may come again. After all, Humpty Dumpty fell off the wall, and yet he married the princess in the end."

"Who is Humpty Dumpty?" asked the little mice.

And then the tree related the whole story, and the little mice were so delighted with it that they were ready to jump to the top of the tree.

The next night a great many more mice made their appearance. On Sunday two rats came, too. But they said that "Humpty Dumpty" was not a pretty story at all.

"Do you know only one story?" asked the rats.

"Only one," replied the fir tree. "I heard it on the happiest evening of my life. But I did not know I was so happy at the time."

"We think it is a miserable story," said the rats. "Don't you know a story about bacon in the storeroom?"

"No," replied the tree.

"Many thanks to you, then," replied the rats, and off they marched.

The little mice also kept away after this, and the tree sighed and said, "It was very pleasant when the merry little mice sat around me and listened while I talked. Now that has passed too. However, I shall consider myself happy when someone comes to take me out of this place."

But would that ever happen? Yes! One morning some people came to clear out the attic. The boxes were packed away, and the tree was pulled from the corner and dragged roughly out upon the staircase, where the daylight shone.

"Life is beginning again," said the tree, rejoicing in the sunshine and fresh air. Then it was carried downstairs and taken into the courtyard so quickly that it forgot to think of itself and could only look about. There was much to be seen. The courtyard was close to a garden, where flowers and trees were blooming. Fresh and fragrant roses hung over the little palings. The swallows flew here and there, crying, "Tweet, tweet, tweet!"

"Now I shall live," cried the tree, joyfully spreading out its branches. But alas! Its branches were all withered and yellow, and the fir tree lay in a corner among weeds and nettles. The star of gold tinsel still stuck in the top of the tree, glittering in the sunshine.

In the courtyard two of the merry children who had danced around the tree at Christmas were playing. The youngest saw the gilded star and pulled it off the tree.

"Look what is sticking to the ugly old fir tree," said the child, treading on the branches till they crackled under his boots. The fir tree saw all the fresh bright flowers in the garden, and then looked at itself, wishing it had remained hidden in the dark corner of the attic.

It thought of its youth in the forest, of the merry Christmas evening, and of the little mice who had listened to the story of Humpty Dumpty.

"Past! Past!" said the old tree. "Oh, had I but enjoyed myself while I could have done so! But now it is too late."

Then a lad came and chopped the tree into pieces, throwing them into a heap on the ground. The pieces were placed in a fire under the pot, and they quickly blazed up brightly, while the tree sighed so deeply that each sigh was like a pistol shot.

Then the children, who were at play, came and sat in front of the fire and looked at it and cried, "Pop, pop!" along with the tree. But each "pop" that the tree made was really a sigh. The tree was thinking of the summer days in the forest, of Christmas evening, and of Humpty Dumpty, the only story it had ever heard or knew how to relate, till at last it was consumed.

The boys went back to play in the garden, the youngest still wearing on his breast the golden star the tree had worn during the happiest evening of its life.

Now all was past. The tree's life was past, and this story, also. For, at last, all stories must come to an end.

The End

Handed down from generation to generation,
the tale of three trees that serve in God's mysterious plan
has been told and retold at Christmas and Easter—
from the pulpit, from the rocking chair,
and always from the heart.

❦

This gentle retelling of the traditional story
places three prayerful children at the heart of the tale,
adding to its wonder and appeal for all listeners,
from age 4 to 104.

When you shall come to the land you shall plant trees.

— Leviticus 19:23 —

A Story of Three Trees

—and the miracle of prayer—

As Told by Steven Robinson

Illustrated by Dave Henderson

Long, long ago, three trees stood on a windswept hillside overlooking a vale of wildflowers.

One was a gentle almond tree, long past its fruit-bearing years. One was a sturdy oak, with wide-reaching branches shaped by soft breezes and strong gales. And one was a mighty cedar, tall and proud.

The trees had watched over the vale for many years, braving the storms of summer, sleeping through snows of winter. They had been planted more than one hundred years before.

Three children had carried the three saplings up that windswept hill.

&

Each child dug a hole and placed a tree in the ground, then covered it with soil. And each child was filled with wonder and hope for the trees and their future.

The first child patted down the earth and said, "Dear God, I pray this almond tree blooms early every spring, bringing joy and cheer. I pray that it bears sweet almonds. And I pray that some day its beautiful wood is carved into a delicate box to hold a precious treasure."

The second child tapped his foot around the base of his sapling and said, "God, I pray that this little oak tree will grow to have a strong heart and spreading branches to protect the little almond tree. I pray that some day its wood may be used to build a royal ship bearing a king."

The third child listened to the others, then slowly took his place alongside his little tree. The other two children stepped back, giving him his space and time.

"I hope and dream," he said quietly, "that this small tree will grow and grow and grow until it reaches the clouds and points skyward toward God. I pray that all who stand here in the years to come will follow its branches into the heavens and feel that God is present and always watching over them."

As the trees grew, they held the words of the three children in their hearts and hoped that some day the prayers would be answered.

And it came to be that one morning a group of woodsmen climbed to the knoll where the trees stood. The woodsmen saw what fine trees they were. "The wood of these trees could be useful," they said.

The first woodsman looked over the gnarled, aged almond tree. "I will use this old wood to build a new feed trough for my cattle," he said.

The tree's heart was sad. It would not become a beautiful treasure box.

The second woodsman raised his axe. "I will use this oak wood to make a fishing boat."

The great oak was felled — and he felt a loss. A fishing boat would never carry a king.

The third woodsman looked up, up, up at the tall, straight cedar tree.

"Cedar is prized for burning offerings," he said. "I will store this lumber and wait for a good price."

The majestic cedar fell with a heavy heart. No longer would he stand on a hill, pointing toward God for all to see.

And so it was, a season later — a hundred years after three small children had planted three small trees — that a young man and woman sought shelter in a stable. There the woman bore a baby boy. She wrapped the baby and placed him on a bed of hay in a feed trough — a lowly manger.

A heavenly light shone through the stable window, wrapping the baby and the manger in gold.

"God is watching over this child," thought the heart of the almond tree. "I am a cradle, and in my arms I hold God's most precious treasure."

Thirty years after this, an old fishing boat carried several men across a large lake. One of the fishermen fell asleep to the gentle rocking of the water. Suddenly, a violent wind blew in. Water started to fill the boat, and the terrified men woke the sleeping man.

This man slowly stood and spread wide his arms.
"Peace! Be still," he said.
And the wind ceased, and there was a great calm.

The men looked at each other.
"What kind of man is this," they said, "that even the wind and the sea obey him?"

But the heart of the oak tree knew. He was carrying the greatest of kings.

All these years, the fragrant cedar wood had lain stacked in a shed, unnoticed, unneeded — until one day when rough hands picked up two large boards and carried them out to the city square. There they were fashioned into a huge cross.

The heavy cross was carried through a crowded street and on up to a lonely hilltop. A quiet, wounded man was laid upon the cross. The heart of the cedar could feel the pain of nails driven into its wood.

And then the cross and man were lifted upright.

"I am pointing again to heaven," thought the cedar, "but God is not here. Only cruelty, pain, and sorrow."

B

ut then the quiet man spoke.

"Father, forgive them, for they know not what they do."

The heart of the great cedar tree was suddenly touched by a peaceful understanding. Only the loving spirit of God could pray such a prayer.

And it knew then that the cross and the holy man it bore would forever point the way to God.

In God's time, in God's way, prayers are answered. Three children smile down through heaven's window and know that this is true.

Joy to the World

Words: Isaac Watts, 1719

Music: Lowell Mason

Joy to the world, the Lord is come! Let
Joy to the earth, the Sav - ior reigns! Let
He rules the world with truth and grace, And

earth re - ceive her King; Let
men their songs em - ploy, While
makes the na - tions prove The

ev - 'ry heart pre - pare Him room, And
fields and floods, rocks, hills and plains Re -
glo - ries of His right - eous - ness, And

Heav-en and na - ture sing, And Heav-en and na - ture sing, And
peat the sound-ing joy, Re - peat the sound-ing joy, Re -
won - ders of His love, And won - ders of His love, And

Heav - en, and Heav - en and na - ture sing.
peat, re - peat the sound - ing joy.
won - ders, won - ders of His love.

Little Women

Excerpts from the chapters "Playing Pilgrims" and "A Merry Christmas"
from the original story by Louisa May Alcott, 1868.
Illustrations by Martin Hargreaves and Lee Wing Painting Workshop.

"Christmas won't be Christmas without any presents," grumbled Jo, lying on the rug.

"It's so dreadful to be poor!" sighed Meg, looking down at her old dress.

"I don't think it's fair for some girls to have plenty of pretty things, and other girls nothing at all," added little Amy, with an injured sniff.

"We've got Father and Mother, and each other, anyhow," said Beth contentedly from her corner.

The four young faces on which the firelight shone brightened at the cheerful words, but darkened again as Jo said sadly, "We haven't got Father, and shall not have him for a long time." She didn't say "perhaps never," but each silently added it, thinking of Father far away, where the fighting* was.

Nobody spoke for a minute; then Meg said in an altered tone, "You know the reason Mother proposed not having any presents this Christmas was because it is going to be a hard winter for everyone; and she thinks we ought not to spend money for pleasure, when our men are suffering so in the army. We can't do much, but we can make our little sacrifices, and ought to do it gladly. But I am afraid I don't." And Meg shook her head, as she thought regretfully of all the pretty things she wanted.

"But I don't think the little we should spend would do any good. We've each got a dollar, and the army wouldn't be much helped by our giving that. I agree not to expect anything from Mother or you, but I do want to buy *Undine and Sintram* for myself. I've wanted it *so* long," said Jo, who was a bookworm.

"I planned to spend mine in new music," said Beth, with a little sigh, which no one heard but the hearth brush and kettle holder.

"I shall get a nice box of Faber's drawing pencils. I really need them," said Amy decidedly.

"Mother didn't say anything about our money, and she won't wish us to give up everything. Let's each buy what we want, and have a little fun. I'm sure we work hard enough to earn it," cried Jo.

The clock struck six and, having swept up the hearth, Beth put a pair of slippers down to warm. Somehow the sight of the old shoes had a good effect upon the girls, for Mother was coming, and everyone brightened to welcome her.

fighting: War Between the States,
    or American Civil War, 1861–1865

170

"They are quite worn out. Marmee must have a new pair," said Jo.

"I thought I'd get her some with my dollar," said Beth.

"No, I shall!" cried Amy.

"I'm the oldest," began Meg, but Jo cut in with a decided:

"I'm the man of the family now Papa is away, and *I* shall provide the slippers, for he told me to take special care of Mother while he was gone."

"I'll tell you what we'll do," said Beth. "Let's each get her something for Christmas, and not get anything for ourselves."

"That's like you, dear! What will we get?" exclaimed Jo.

Everyone thought soberly for a minute, then Meg announced, as if the idea was suggested by the sight of her own pretty hands, "I shall give her a nice pair of gloves."

"Army shoes, best to be had," cried Jo.

"Some handkerchiefs, all hemmed," said Beth.

"I'll get a little bottle of cologne. She likes it, and it won't cost much, so I'll have some left to buy my pencils," added Amy.

"How will we give the things?" asked Meg.

"Put them on the table, and bring her in and see her open the bundles. Don't you remember how we used to do on our birthdays?" answered Jo.

"I used to be *so* frightened when it was my turn to sit in the big chair with the crown on, and see you all come marching round to give the presents, with a kiss. I liked the things and the kisses, but it was dreadful to have you sit looking at me while I opened the bundles," said Beth, who was toasting her face and the bread for tea at the same time.

"Let Marmee think we are getting things for ourselves, and then surprise her. We must go shopping tomorrow afternoon, Meg. There is so much to do about the play for Christmas night," said Jo, marching up and down, with her hands behind her back, and her nose in the air.

"Glad to find you so merry, my girls," said a cheery voice at the door, and actors and audience turned to welcome a tall, motherly lady with a "can-I-help-you" look about her which was truly delightful. She was not elegantly dressed, but a noble-looking woman, and the girls thought the gray cloak and unfashionable bonnet covered the most splendid mother in the world.

"Well, dearies, how have you got on today? There was so much to do, getting the boxes ready to go tomorrow, that I didn't come home to dinner. Has anyone called, Beth? How is your cold, Meg? Jo, you look tired to death. Come and kiss me, baby."

As they gathered about the table, Mrs. March said, with a particularly happy face, "I've got a treat for you after supper."

A quick, bright smile went round like a streak of sunshine. Beth clapped her hands, regardless of the biscuit she held, and Jo tossed up her napkin, crying, "A letter! A letter! Three cheers for Father!"

"Yes, a nice long letter. He is well, and thinks he shall get through the cold season better than we feared. He sends all sorts of loving wishes for Christmas, and an especial message to you girls," said Mrs. March, patting her pocket as if she had got a treasure there.

"When will he come home, Marmee?" asked Beth, with a little quiver in her voice.

"Not for many months, dear, unless he is sick. He will stay and do his work faithfully as long as he can, and we won't ask for him back a minute sooner than he can be spared. Now come and hear the letter."

It was a cheerful, hopeful letter, full of lively descriptions of camp life, marches, and military news, and only at the end did the writer's heart overflow with fatherly love and longing for the little girls at home.

"Give them all of my dear love and a kiss. Tell them I think of them by day, pray for them by night, and find my best comfort in their affection at all times. A year seems very long to wait before I see them, but remind them that while we wait we may all work, so that these hard days need not be wasted. I know they will remember all I said to them, that they will be loving children to you, will do their duty faithfully, fight their bosom enemies bravely, and conquer themselves so beautifully that when I come back to them I may be fonder and prouder than ever of my little women."

Mrs. March broke the silence that followed . . . by saying in her cheery voice, "Do you remember how you used to play *Pilgrim's Progress** when you were little things? Nothing delighted you more than to have me tie my piece bags on your backs for burdens, give you hats and sticks and rolls of paper, and let you travel through the house from the cellar, which was the City of Destruction, up, up, to the housetop, where you had all the lovely things you could collect to make a Celestial City. ... Look under your pillows Christmas morning, and you will find your guidebook."

Pilgrim's Progress: game based on the John Bunyan book, which includes the pilgrim Christian, as well as a City of Destruction, Celestial City, and Slough of Despond

Jo was the first to wake in the gray dawn of Christmas morning. No stockings hung at the fireplace, and for a moment she felt as much disappointed as she did long ago, when her little sock fell down because it was crammed so full of goodies. Then she remembered her mother's promise and, slipping her hand under her pillow, drew out a little crimson-covered book. She knew it very well, for it was that beautiful old story of the best life ever lived, and Jo felt that it was a true guidebook for any pilgrim going on a long journey. She woke Meg with a "Merry Christmas," and bade her see what was under her pillow. A green-covered book appeared, with the same picture inside, and a few words written by their mother, which made their one present very precious in their eyes. Presently Beth and Amy woke to rummage and find their little books also, one dove-colored, the other blue—and all sat looking at and talking about them, while the east grew rosy with the coming day.

"I'm glad mine is blue," said Amy; and then the rooms were very still while the pages were softly turned, and the winter sunshine crept in to touch the bright heads and serious faces with a Christmas greeting.

"Where is Mother?" asked Meg, as she and Jo ran down to thank her for their gifts, half an hour later.

"Goodness only knows. Some poor creeter came a-beggin', and your ma went straight off to see what was needed. There never *was* such a woman for givin' away vittles and drink, clothes and firin'," replied Hannah, who had lived with the family since Meg was born, and was considered by them all more as a friend than a servant.

"She will be back soon, I think, so fry your cakes, and have everything ready," said Meg, looking over the presents which were collected in a basket and kept under the sofa, ready to be produced at the proper time

"Merry Christmas, Marmee! Many of them! Thank you for our books. We read some, and mean to every day," they all cried in chorus.

"Merry Christmas, little daughters! I'm glad you began at once, and hope you will keep on. But I want to say one word before we sit down. Not far away from here lies a poor woman with a little newborn baby. Six children are huddled into one bed to keep from freezing, for they have no fire. There is nothing to eat over there, and the oldest boy came to tell me they were suffering hunger and cold. My girls, will you give them your breakfast as a Christmas present?"

They were all unusually hungry, having waited nearly an hour, and for a minute no one spoke— only a minute, for Jo exclaimed impetuously, "I'm so glad you came before we began!"

"May I go and help carry the things to the poor little children?" asked Beth eagerly.

"*I* shall take the cream and the muffins," added Amy, heroically giving up the article she most liked.

Meg was already covering the buckwheats, and piling the bread into one big plate.

"I thought you'd do it," said Mrs. March, smiling as if satisfied. "You shall all go and help me, and when we come back we will have bread and milk for breakfast, and make it up at dinnertime."

They were soon ready, and the procession set out. Fortunately it was early, and they went through back streets, so few people saw them, and no one laughed at the queer party.

A poor, bare, miserable room it was, with broken windows, no fire, ragged bedclothes, a sick mother, wailing baby, and a group of pale, hungry children cuddled under one old quilt, trying to keep warm.

How the big eyes stared and the blue lips smiled as the girls went in!

"*Ach, mein Gott!* It is good angels come to us!" said the poor woman, crying for joy.

"Funny angels in hoods and mittens," said Jo, and set them to laughing.

In a few minutes it really did seem as if kind spirits had been at work there. Hannah, who had carried wood, made a fire, and stopped up the broken panes with old hats and her own cloak. Mrs. March gave the mother tea and gruel, and comforted her with promises of help, while she dressed the little baby as tenderly as if it had been her own. The girls meantime spread the table, set the children round the fire, and fed them like so many hungry birds—laughing, talking, and trying to understand the funny broken English.

"*Das ist gut!*" "*Die Engel-kinder!*" cried the poor things as they ate and warmed their purple hands at the comfortable blaze.

The girls had never been called "angel children" before, and thought it very agreeable, especially Jo, who had been considered a "Sancho" ever since she was born. That was a very happy breakfast, though they didn't get any of it; and when they went away, leaving comfort behind, I think there were not in all the city four merrier people than the hungry little girls who gave away their breakfasts and contented themselves with bread and milk on Christmas morning.

"That's loving our neighbor better than ourselves, and I like it," said Meg, as they set out their presents while their mother was upstairs collecting clothes for the poor Hummels.

Not a very splendid show, but there was a great deal of love done up in the few little bundles, and the tall vase of red roses, white chrysanthemums, and trailing vines, which stood in the middle, gave quite an elegant air to the table.

"She's coming! Strike up, Beth! Open the door, Amy! Three cheers for Marmee!" cried Jo, prancing about while Meg went to conduct Mother to the seat of honor.

Beth played her gayest march, Amy threw open the door, and Meg enacted escort with great dignity. Mrs. March was both surprised and touched, and smiled with her eyes full as she examined her presents and read the little notes which accompanied them. The slippers went on at once, a new handkerchief was slipped into her pocket, well scented with Amy's cologne, the rose was fastened in her bosom, and the nice gloves were pronounced a "perfect fit."

There was a good deal of laughing and kissing and explaining, in the simple, loving fashion which makes these home festivals so pleasant at the time, so sweet to remember long afterward....

Hark! the Herald Angels Sing

Words: Charles Wesley, 1739

Music: Felix Mendelssohn, 1840

Hark! the her - ald an - gels sing,___ "Glo - ry to the
Hail the heav'n - born Prince of Peace!___ Hail the Sun of

new - born King; Peace on Earth, and mer - cy mild,___
Right - eous - ness! Light and life to all He brings,___

God and sin - ners re - con - ciled!" Joy - ful, all ye
Ris'n with heal - ing in His wings. Mild He lays His

na - tions, rise,___ Join the tri - umph of the skies;___
glo - ry by,___ Born that man no more may die.___

With an - ge - lic host pro - claim, "Christ is___ born in
Born to raise the sons of earth, Born to___ give them

Beth - le - hem!" Hark! the her - ald an - gels sing,
se - cond birth. Hark! the her - ald an - gels sing,

"Glo - ry___ to the new - born King!"
"Glo - ry___ to the new - born King!"

A CHRISTMAS CAROL

Adapted from "Tiny Tim" in Boys and Girls of Bookland,
written by Nora Archibald Smith.
Original story by Charles Dickens, 1843.
Facing illustration by Jessie Willcox Smith • Drawings by Jason Alexander.

A CHRISTMAS CAROL, by Charles Dickens, is one of the most famous of all Christmas tales. In many households it is read aloud by the fireside every Christmas season, and people hear it through a mist of smiles and tears. It has the very breath and spirit of Christmas in it, and, as you read, the walls dress themselves with holly, mistletoe hangs in the doorway, church bells ring and sleigh bells tinkle out-of-doors, and on the frosty air come floating delicious odors of plum pudding, red-hot chestnuts, spicy mince pies, cherry-cheeked apples, luscious grapes, and slowly browning turkey.

Timothy Cratchit, youngest child of Robert Cratchit, is but one tiny figure in the story—and yet his is the face we love the best in the book, and the one that comes most clearly to us when the Christmas carols sound. You can see him in the picture, standing by his father at the Christmas service—fair-haired, blue-eyed, with just a hint of rose in his cheeks as he joins in the singing of:

> *Hark! the herald angels sing,*
> *"Glory to the newborn King!"*

His little crutch stands beside him in the pew, for he is lame. Still, he is a happy lad, for he has a good and loving father and mother and a bevy of brothers and sisters.

If there is any hero in the book, I suppose it is Scrooge, Ebenezer Scrooge, the employer of Tim's father, though it is hard to make a hero out of a man whose very name sounds like a creaking door, or a dull saw trying to cut through a tough plank. We have it on Dickens' own written word that Scrooge was a "squeezing, wrenching, grasping, scraping, clutching, covetous old sinner," and that he was "hard and sharp as flint, secret and self-contained, and solitary as an oyster!"

Ebenezer Scrooge was Bob Cratchit's employer, as before said, and Bob was the father of tiny, crippled Tim, of Martha, of Belinda, of Peter, and also of two middle-sized Cratchits. That was a large family to keep, even had Mr. Cratchit's been an equally large salary; but, as it was, it is no wonder that poor Bob never could afford an overcoat, but wore instead a white comforter around his neck, closely wrapped, with the ends hanging down below his waist.

The book begins on Christmas Eve, in Mr. Scrooge's office. Mr. Scrooge is cross—wishing there were no such day as Christmas, fiercely refusing his nephew's invitation to dinner, grudging poor Bob his holiday at home, and declining to give one penny to some gentlemen who come to ask him for a donation for the poor.

Satisfied with having made everybody about him unhappy, Scrooge went home to his lonely house and his lonely room; and by-and-by, while he was still minding his own business, the Ghost of Christmas Past came to his bedside!

Of course Scrooge was afraid; not because the Spirit wore a frightful form, for indeed his face was fair, and he bore a sprig of greenest holly in his hand. No, it was not that; but because the unearthly visitant proclaimed that he was the Ghost of Christmas Past, and would bear Scrooge through the window and abroad upon the air to visit again the scenes of his boyhood.

Only the day before he had growled in his office: "Out upon Merry Christmas! A fig for the Season! What's Christmas time to me?" and now he was to see what it had been to him in youth, and so refresh his withered heart with the dews of memory.

Scrooge and the Spirit soared above the little town where he was born, and saw the merry boys on their shaggy ponies, laughing and shouting, and calling Christmas greetings to one another as they parted at the crossroads for their several homes. They saw the old boarding school where Scrooge had been left once for the holidays, and the lonely boy sitting there without companions, except for those in the books he was reading. They saw the long-dead little sister running to throw her arms about his neck and to tell him they were to spend Christmas together.

Scrooge felt it all—oh, yes, he remembered it—and when the Spirit looked on him intently, he saw a tear upon Scrooge's furrowed cheek.

When the journey was over, Scrooge sank to sleep again in his own bed, and never wakened till the neighboring church struck ONE! when, not much to his surprise, for nothing could surprise him now, he found that he lay in a blaze of ruddy light that streamed from the adjoining room. Creeping softly to the door and peeping in, he saw a jolly Giant, robed in green, a holly wreath upon his curls, bearing in his hand a glowing torch shaped like Plenty's horn.

"I am the Ghost of Christmas Present," cried the figure. "Hold fast to my robe and we will fare abroad and see how the world keeps holiday at this most blessed time of all the year."

Scrooge had learned many things of the Ghost of Christmas Past, and now he was ready to follow the new Spirit wherever he might go.

In a moment they stood in the winter streets, and saw the people shoveling away the snow and calling Merry Christmas to their neighbors. They saw the grocers' and fruit-sellers' windows, overflowing with dainties. They heard the bells ringing, and saw the families trooping to church. And then they soared on high, far over the land, and saw that in shepherds' huts upon the moors, deep down in mines, in lonely lighthouses, on ships at sea, even in prisons and among the convicts, there was no man who had not a kinder word for another on that day and who had not remembered those he cared for with a warmer heart.

They went to many poor and humble houses, too, but to none among them all happier than Bob Cratchit's—Scrooge's ill-paid clerk. Bob and Tiny Tim had gone to church, but everybody else was at home either preparing dinner, expecting dinner, talking about dinner, or smelling dinner!

Then in came Bob with Tiny Tim upon his shoulder. Of course great rejoicing followed over the united family, and presently Tim was borne off by the two middle-sized Cratchits that he might hear the Christmas pudding singing as it boiled.

"And how did little Tim behave at church?" asked Mrs. Cratchit.

"As good as gold," said Bob, "and better. Somehow he gets thoughtful, sitting by himself so much, and thinks the strangest things you ever heard. He told me, coming home, that he hoped the people saw him in the church, because he was a cripple, and it might be pleasant for them to remember, upon Christmas Day, Who made lame beggars walk and blind men see."

The father, and the mother, too, were a little tremulous and tearful as Tim's words were repeated, for indeed the little lad was far from strong, but in a moment the tap of his crutch was heard, and it was announced that dinner was ready!

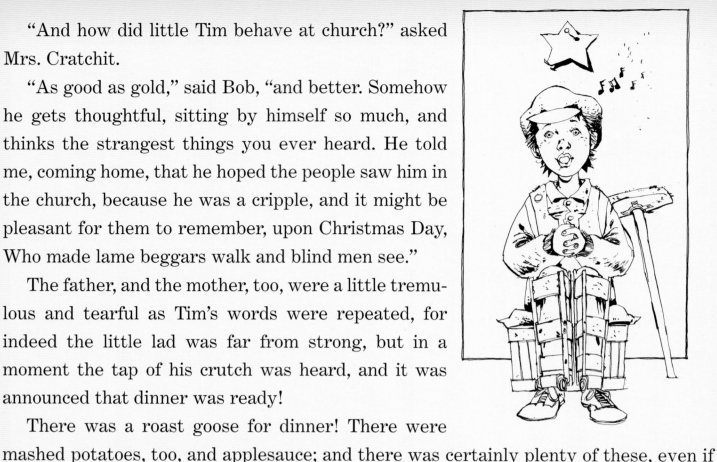

There was a roast goose for dinner! There were mashed potatoes, too, and applesauce; and there was certainly plenty of these, even if the goose was not so very big. And then there was a plum pudding—a perfectly wonderful pudding—and everybody admired it and exclaimed about it and feasted on it, and nobody said or thought that it was at all a small pudding for such a large family. "Any Cratchit would have blushed to hint at such a thing!"

You can fancy how old Scrooge felt while he and the Spirit looked upon these things, and how he marveled at the happiness the Day had brought to these humble people. He noted Tiny Tim especially, sitting by his father's side when the dinner was over, and when Bob cried: "A Merry Christmas to us all, my dears; God bless us," he heard, with tears, how Tim echoed:

"God bless us, every one!"

"The little lad seems very frail," said Scrooge to the Spirit anxiously. "Tell me if he will live!"

"I see a vacant seat," replied the Ghost, "in the poor chimney-corner, and a crutch without an owner, carefully preserved. If these shadows remain unaltered by the Future, the child will die."

"No, no," said Scrooge. "Oh, no, kind Spirit! say he will be spared."

"What is his life to you?" returned the Ghost.

Scrooge bent his head in grief to hear these words, and, as he did so, the Ghost of Christmas Present passed from sight.

Trembling with fear and with anxiety, the old man awaited in an open place the last of the Spirits—the Ghost of Christmas Yet-to-Come. He had learned much from the two former phantoms; his heart had begun to beat again, and he had begun to see more clearly what life might be in the future, not only to him but to those about him, but he dreaded that it was too late to change his fate.

"Ghost of the Future!" Scrooge exclaimed, "I fear you more than any specter I have seen. But I know your purpose is to do me good. Will you not speak to me?"

The Spirit, shrouded in a deep black garment which concealed its face and form, made no reply but pointed onward, and Scrooge followed in the shadow of its dress, which seemed to bear him up.

They passed along the streets of London, and here and there heard men discussing the death of some old curmudgeon of a merchant for whom nobody seemed to care and to whose funeral nobody seemed willing to go.

At last they entered poor Bob Cratchit's house and found the mother and children seated round the fire—but quiet, very quiet. The mother was sewing on some black material, but she laid her work upon the table suddenly and put her hand up to her face, saying the color hurt her eyes. "Is it not time for your father, children?" she asked.

"Past it, rather," Peter answered; "but I think he's walked a little slower than he used, these last few evenings, Mother."

"I have known him to walk," said Mother, "very fast—with Tim upon his shoulder—very fast indeed. But Tim was very light to carry, and his father loved him so that it was no trouble—never any trouble."

When Bob came in, Scrooge saw at once what had happened, and saw it with an aching heart. No Tiny Tim was there to meet Bob, and as soon as he had sat down, the two middle-sized Cratchits got upon his knees and laid each child a little cheek against his face, as if they said, "Don't mind it, Father; don't be grieved!"

The tears were so thick in Scrooge's eyes that he could hardly see, and his sobs shook him so that he followed the Spirit with difficulty as he sped away from that grief-stricken house, away, away to a lonely graveyard where, upon a neglected stone the carved letters EBENEZER SCROOGE were plainly to be seen.

Scrooge fell upon his knees before the Phantom at this sight. "I am not the man I was!" he cried. "Assure me that I yet may change these shadows you have shown me by an altered life. I will honor Christmas in my heart, and try to keep it all the year. Have pity upon me, Spirit, that these things may not befall!"

He still knelt, holding up his hands in eager supplication, when he seemed to see an alteration in the Phantom's hood and dress. It shrank, collapsed, and, wonder of wonders, it dwindled down to his own bedpost!

Yes, it really was his own bedpost. "The bed was his own, the room was his own, and, best and happiest of all, the time before him was his own, to make amends in. He scrambled out of bed, so happy that he could hardly stand. He rushed to the window, and there were the churches ringing out the lustiest peals he had ever heard: 'Clash, clang, hammer, ding, dong, bell. Bell, dong, ding, hammer, clang, clash. Oh, glorious, glorious!'"

"What day is this?" cried Scrooge to a boy in the street below.

"What!" returned the boy, with all his might of wonder. "Why, CHRISTMAS DAY!"

"Christmas Day!" thought Scrooge. "Then the Spirits must have done it all in one night. Why, it's wonderful! I can begin all over again!"

And he did begin all over again, and he did it immediately. He asked the boy in the street that very minute to go and buy the prize turkey at the corner and take it to the Cratchits'; he met in the square, when he went out, the very gentlemen who had asked him for help for the poor the previous day, and gave them such a sum that they nearly fainted where they stood; he went to his nephew's to dinner, and was the life of the party.

And next morning, Scrooge was waiting in the counting-house when Bob Cratchit came, and raised his salary before the astonished fellow could wink.

Oh, no, indeed, Tiny Tim did not die; and by-and-by Scrooge was a second father to him and a help to all the family.

In fact, "Scrooge became as good a friend, as good a master, and as good a man as the good old city of London ever knew." It was always said of him, thereafter, that he knew how to keep Christmas well, if any man alive possessed the knowledge.

May that be truly said of us, and all of us! And so, as Tiny Tim observed:

"God Bless Us, Every One!"

We Wish You a Merry Christmas

English Traditional

We wish you a Mer - ry Christ - mas! We
Oh, bring us a fig - gy pud - ding! Oh,
We won't go un - til we get some! We
We wish you a Mer - ry Christ - mas! We

wish you a Mer - ry Christ - mas! We wish you a Mer - ry
bring us a fig - gy pud - ding! Oh, bring us a fig - gy
won't go un - til we get some! We won't go un - til we
wish you a Mer - ry Christ - mas! We wish you a Mer - ry

Christ - mas, and a Hap - py New Year! Good
pud - ding, and a cup of good cheer!
get some, so bring some right here! We
Christ - mas, and a Hap - py New Year!

tid - ings we bring to you and your

kin; Good tid - ings for Christ - mas and a

Hap - py New Year!

The Wind in the Willows

Exerpts of the chapter "Dulce Domum"
from the original story by Kenneth Grahame, 1908.
Illustrated by Nick Price and Lee Wing Painting Workshop

Ratty and Mole were returning across country after a long day's outing with Otter.

"Ratty!" Mole called, full of joyful excitement, "hold on! Come back! I want you, quick!"

"Oh, *come* along, Mole, *do*!" replied the Rat cheerfully, still plodding along.

"*Please* stop, Ratty!" pleaded the poor Mole, in anguish of heart. "You don't understand! It's my home, my old home! I've just come across the smell of it, and it's close by here, really quite close. And I *must* go to it, I must, I must! Oh, come back, Ratty! Please, please come back!"

"We're going to find that home of yours, old fellow," replied the Rat pleasantly; "so you had better come along, for it will take some finding, and we shall want your nose."

The Rat, much excited, kept close to his heels as the Mole, with something of the air of a sleep-walker, crossed a dry ditch, scrambled through a hedge, and nosed his way over a field open and trackless and bare in the faint starlight.

Suddenly, without giving warning, he dived; but the Rat was on the alert, and promptly followed him down the tunnel to which his unerring nose had faithfully led him.

Mole's face beamed at the sight of all these objects so dear to him, and he hurried Rat through the door, lit a lamp in the hall, and took one glance round his old home. He saw the dust lying thick on everything, saw the cheerless, deserted look of the long-neglected house, and its narrow, meager dimensions, its worn and shabby contents—and collapsed again on a hall chair, his nose in his paws. "Oh, Ratty!" he cried dismally, "why ever did I do it? Why did I bring you to this poor, cold little place, on a night like this, when you might have been at River Bank by this time, toasting your toes before a blazing fire, with all your own nice things about you!"

The Rat paid no heed to his doleful self-reproaches. He was running here and there, opening doors, inspecting rooms and cupboards, and lighting lamps and candles and sticking them up everywhere. "What a capital little house this is!" he called out cheerily. "So compact! So well planned! Everything here and everything in its place! We'll make a jolly night of it. The first thing we want is a good fire; I'll see to that—I always know where to find things. So this is the parlor? Splendid! Your own idea, those little sleeping bunks in the wall? Capital! Now, I'll fetch the wood and the coals, and you get a duster, Mole—you'll find one in the drawer of the kitchen table—and try and smarten things up a bit. Bustle about, old chap!"

Sounds were heard from the forecourt without—sounds like the scuffling of small feet in the gravel and a confused murmur of tiny voices, while broken sentences reached them—"Now, all in a line—hold the lantern up a bit, Tommy—clear your throats first—no coughing after I say one, two, three.—Where's young Bill?—Here, come on, do, we're all a-waiting—"

"What's up?" inquired the Rat, pausing in his labors.

"I think it must be the fieldmice," replied the Mole, with a touch of pride in his manner. "They go round carol-singing regularly at this time of the year."

"Let's have a look at them!" cried the Rat, jumping up and running to the door.

It was a pretty sight, and a seasonable one, that met their eyes when they flung the door open. In the forecourt, lit by the dim rays of a horn lantern, some eight or ten little fieldmice stood in a semicircle, red worsted comforters round their throats, their forepaws thrust deep into their pockets, their feet jigging for warmth. With bright beady eyes they glanced shyly at each other, sniggering a little, sniffing and applying coat-sleeves a good deal. As the door opened, one of the elder ones that carried the lantern was just saying, "Now, then, one, two, three!" and forthwith their shrill little voices uprose on the air, singing one of the old-time carols that their forefathers composed in fields that were fallow and held by frost, or when snowbound in chimney corners, and handed down to be sung in the miry street to lamplit windows at Yule time.

Carol

Villagers all, this frosty tide,
Let your doors swing open wide,
Though wind may follow, and snow beside,
Yet draw us in by your fire to bide;
  Joy shall be yours in the morning!

Here we stand in the cold and the sleet,
Blowing fingers and stamping feet,
Come from far away you to greet—
You by the fire and we in the street—
  Bidding you joy in the morning!

For ere one half of the night was gone,
Sudden a star has led us on,
Raining bliss and benison— *
Bliss tomorrow and more anon,
  Joy for every morning!

Goodman Joseph toiled through the snow—
Saw the star o'er a stable low;
Mary she might not further go—
Welcome thatch, and litter below!
  Joy was hers in the morning!

And then they heard the angels tell
"Who were the first to cry *Noel*?
Animals all, as it befell,
In the stable where they did dwell!
  Joy shall be theirs in the morning!"

benison: blessing

192

The voices ceased, the singers, bashful but smiling, exchanged sidelong glances, and silence succeeded—but for a moment only. Then, from up above and far away, down the tunnel they had so lately traveled was borne to their ears in a faint musical hum the sound of distant bells ringing a joyful and clangorous peal.

"Very well sung, boys!" cried the Rat heartily. "And now come along in, all of you, and warm yourselves by the fire, and have something hot!"

Under the generalship of Rat, everybody was set to do something or to fetch something. In a very few minutes supper was ready, and Mole, as he took the head of the table in a sort of a dream, saw a lately barren board set thick with savory comforts; saw his little friends' faces brighten and beam as they fell to without delay; and then let himself loose—for he was famished indeed—on the provender so magically provided, thinking what a happy homecoming this had turned out, after all. As they ate, they talked of old times, and the fieldmice gave him the local gossip up to date, and answered as well as they could the hundred questions he had to ask them. The Rat said little or nothing, only taking care that each guest had what he wanted, and plenty of it, and that Mole had no trouble or anxiety about anything.

They clattered off at last, very grateful and showering wishes of the season, with their jacket pockets stuffed with remembrances for the small brothers and sisters at home.

The weary Mole also was glad to turn in without delay, and soon had his head on his pillow, in great joy and contentment. … it was good to think he had this to come back to; this place which was all his own, these things which were so glad to see him again and could always be counted upon for the same simple welcome.

Christmas Lullaby

IN a cradle so dainty,
a warm cozy nest,
Baby, sweet baby, is taking his rest.

Upon the white pillow his pretty head lies;
Closed for the night are his bonnie blue eyes.

The little hand's dimpled and pink as a rose.
And just what he's dreaming of, nobody knows.

Santa peeks at the baby, then leaves him a toy,
A cuddly soft doll for a small baby boy.

Then he tiptoes away, as the wee baby seems
To be floating away on an ocean of dreams.

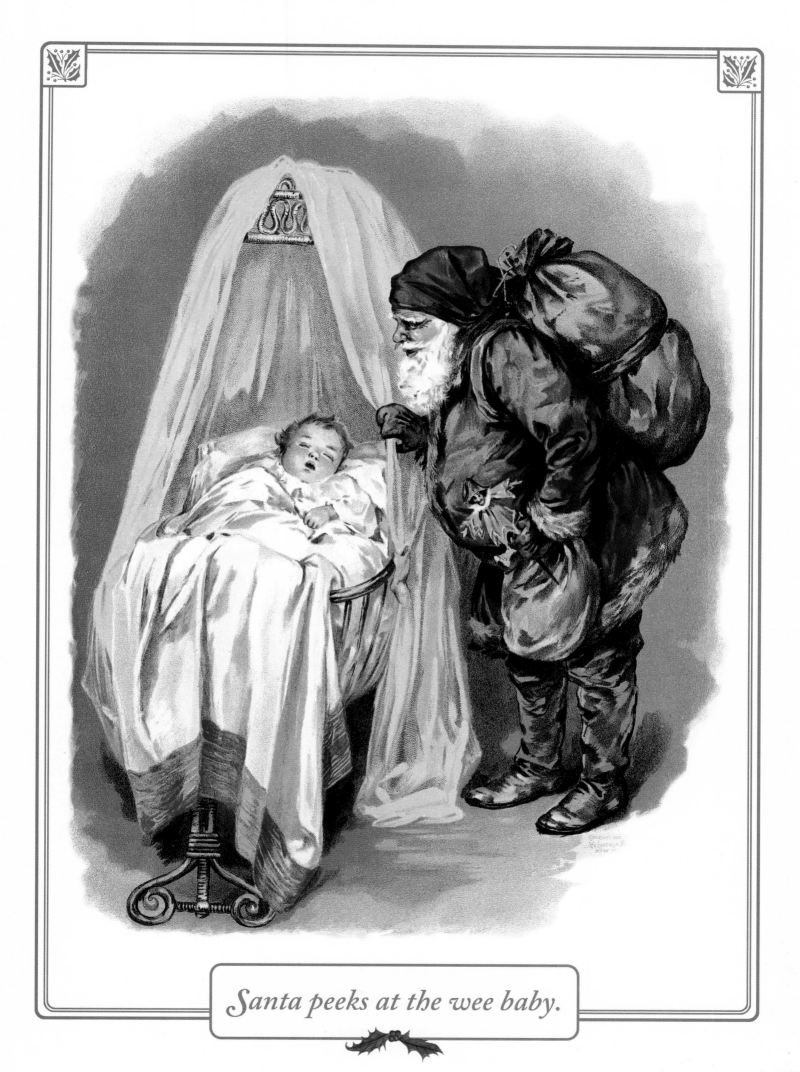

Santa peeks at the wee baby.

Away in a Manger

Verses 1 & 2: Anonymous
Verse 3: John T. McFarland

Music: James Murray

A - way in a man - ger, no
The cat - tle are low - ing, the
Be near me, Lord Je - sus; I

crib for a bed, The lit - tle Lord
ba - by a - wakes, But lit - tle Lord
ask Thee to stay Close by me for -

Je - sus laid down His sweet head. The
Je - sus, no cry - ing He makes. I
ev - er, and love me, I pray. Bless

stars in the sky____ looked down where He
love Thee, Lord Je - sus; look down from the
all the dear chil - dren in Thy ten - der

lay, The lit - tle Lord Je - sus, a -
sky, And stay by my cra - dle till
care, And fit us for Heav - en to

sleep on the hay.
morn - ing is nigh.
live with Thee there.

This is the story of the birth of Jesus
as told in the second chapter of Luke
in the New Testament.

More than two thousand years
have passed since the first Christmas.
And to this day, with joy and gifts and praise,
we celebrate the birth of Jesus,
the most blessed Newborn King.

The
NEWBORN
KING

Illustrated
by Pat Thompson

From the Book of Luke
Adapted by Cindy R. Waters

In ancient times, the Roman ruler ordered a count to be taken of all the people who lived in the Roman Empire. Each person went to the town where he was born to be counted.

A man named Joseph left his home in Nazareth and traveled to Bethlehem. His wife, Mary, who was expecting her first baby, went with him.

While they were in Bethlehem,
Mary gave birth to a baby boy.
They were staying in a stable
because there were no rooms
left for them to rent.

Mary wrapped
the baby in a soft
blanket and placed
him on the straw
in the manger.

Outside the city, shepherds were sleeping in the fields so they could protect their flocks of sheep. God sent an angel to tell the shepherds the great news, but the angel was shining so brightly that the shepherds were afraid.

The angel spoke to the shepherds and told them he was bringing them wonderful news that was for all the people on earth.

"Today in the town of David, a Savior has been born to you; he is Christ the Lord. This will be a sign to you: You will find the baby wrapped in cloth and lying in a manger."

Suddenly more angels
appeared and they were
all praising God and saying,
"Glory to God in the highest,
and on earth peace, good will toward men."

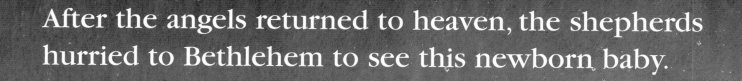

After the angels returned to heaven, the shepherds hurried to Bethlehem to see this newborn baby.

"Let us go to Bethlehem to see this thing that has happened, which the Lord has told us about," they said to one another.

There they found Mary, and Joseph, and the baby,
who was lying in a manger, just as
the angel had told them.

The shepherds were so amazed
by all this that they told everyone
they saw about the blessed new baby.

And all who heard it wondered
at what the shepherds told them.

Mary was happy. She kept these memories and treasured them in her heart.

Returning to the fields, the shepherds were also happy and praising God for all the wonderful things they had heard and seen.

"Glory to **GOD** in the highest,
and on earth peace,
good will toward men."

LUKE 2:14
KJV